The COURAGE *of* CAPTAIN PLUM

By

JAMES OLIVER CURWOOD

AMS PRESS
NEW YORK

"I am going to take you from the island!"—*Page* 158

The COURAGE *of* CAPTAIN PLUM

By
JAMES OLIVER CURWOOD

WITH ILLUSTRATIONS BY
FRANK E. SCHOONOVER

INDIANAPOLIS
THE BOBBS-MERRILL COMPANY
PUBLISHERS

Library of Congress Cataloging in Publication Data

Curwood, James Oliver, 1878-1927.
    The courage of Captain Plum.

    I. Title.
PZ3.C949Cf6 [PS3505.U92]   813'.5'2   71-144593
ISBN 0-404-01895-5

Reprinted from an original copy in the collections of
the University of Virginia Library.

From the edition of 1908, Indianapolis
First AMS edition published in 1972
Manufactured in the United States of America

International Standard Book Number: 0-404-01895-5

AMS PRESS INC.
NEW YORK, N.Y. 10003

The COURAGE *of* CAPTAIN PLUM

THE COURAGE OF CAPTAIN PLUM

CHAPTER I

THE TWO OATHS

On an afternoon in the early summer of 1856 Captain Nathaniel Plum, master and owner of the sloop *Typhoon* was engaged in nothing more important than the smoking of an enormous pipe. Clouds of strongly odored smoke, tinted with the lights of the setting sun, had risen above his head in unremitting volumes for the last half hour. There was infinite contentment in his face, notwithstanding the fact that he had been meditating on a subject that was not altogether pleasant. But Captain Plum was, in a way, a philosopher, though one would

1

not have guessed this **fact** from his appearance. He was, in the first place, a young man, not more than eight or nine and twenty, and his strong, rather thin face, tanned by exposure to the sea, was just now lighted up by eyes that shone with an unbounded good humor which any instant might take the form of laughter.

At the present time Captain Plum's vision was confined to one direction, which carried his gaze out over Lake Michigan. Earlier in the day he had been able to discern the hazy outline of the Michigan wilderness twenty miles to the eastward. Straight ahead, shooting up rugged and sharp in the red light of the day's end, were two islands. Between these, three miles away, the sloop *Typhoon* was strongly silhouetted in the fading glow. Beyond the islands and the sloop there were no other objects for Captain Plum's eyes to rest upon. So far as he could see there was no other sail. At his back he was shut in by a dense growth of trees and creeping vines, and unless a small boat edged close in around the end of Beaver Island his place of concealment must remain undiscovered. At least this seemed an assured fact to Captain Plum.

In the security of his position he began to whistle softly as he beat the bowl of his pipe on his boot-heel to empty it of ashes. Then he drew a long-barreled revolver from under a coat that he had thrown aside and examined it carefully to see that the powder and ball were in solid and that none of the caps was missing. From the same place he brought forth a belt, buckled it round his waist, shoved the revolver into its holster, and dragging the coat to him, fished out a letter from an inside pocket. It was a dirty, much worn letter. Perhaps he had read it a score of times. He read it again now, and then, refilling his pipe, settled back against the rock that formed a rest for his shoulders and turned his eyes in the direction of the sloop.

The last rim of the sun had fallen below the Michigan wilderness and in the rapidly increasing gloom the sloop was becoming indistinguishable. Captain Plum looked at his watch. He must still wait a little longer before setting out upon the adventure that had brought him to this isolated spot. He rested his head against the rock, and thought. He had been thinking for hours. Back in the thicket he heard the prowling of some small animal. There came the sleepy chirp of a bird and the rustling of tired wings settling for the night. A strange stillness hovered about him, and with it there came over him a loneliness that was chilling, a loneliness that made him homesick. It was a new and unpleasant sensation to Captain Plum. He could not remember just when he had experienced it before; that is, if he dated the present from two weeks ago to-night. It was then that the letter had been handed to him in Chicago, and it had been a weight upon his soul and a prick to his conscience ever since. Once or twice he had made up his mind to destroy it, but each time he had repented at the last moment. In a sudden revulsion at his weakness he pulled himself together,

4

crumpled the dirty missive into a ball, and flung it out upon the white rim of beach.

At this action there came a quick movement in the dense wall of verdure behind him. Noiselessly the tangle of vines separated and a head thrust itself out in time to see the bit of paper fall short of the water's edge. Then the head shot back as swiftly and as silently as a serpent's. Perhaps Captain Plum heard the gloating chuckle that followed the movement. If so he thought it only some night bird in the brush.

"Heigh-ho!" he exclaimed with some return of his old cheer, "it's about time we were starting!" He jumped to his feet and began brushing the sand from his clothes. When he had done, he walked out upon the rim of beach and stretched himself until his arm-bones cracked.

Again the hidden head shot forth from its concealment. A sudden turn and Captain Plum would certainly have been startled. For it was a weird object, this spying head; its face dead-white against the dense green of the verdure, with shocks of long white hair hanging down on each side, framing between them a pair of eyes that gleamed from cavernous sockets, like black glowing beads. There was unmistakable fear, a tense anxiety in those glittering eyes as Captain Plum walked toward the paper, but when he paused and stretched himself, the sole of his boot carelessly trampling the discarded letter, the head disappeared again and there came another satisfied bird-like chuckle from the gloom of the thicket.

Captain Plum now put on his coat, buttoned it close to conceal the weapons in his belt, and walked along the narrow water-run that crept like a white ribbon between the lake and the island wilderness. No sooner had he disappeared than the bushes and vines behind the rock were torn asunder and a man wormed his way through them. For an instant he paused, listening for returning footsteps, and then with startling agility darted to the beach and seized the crumpled letter.

6

The person who for the greater part of the
afternoon had been spying upon Captain Plum
from the security of the thicket was to all ap-
pearances a very small and a very old man,
though there was something about him that
seemed to belie a first guess at his age. His
face was emaciated; his hair was white and hung
in straggling masses on his shoulders; his hooked
nose bore apparently the infallible stamp of extreme age. Yet there was a strange and uncanny
strength and quickness in his movements.
There was no stoop to his shoulders. His
head was set squarely. His eyes were as keen
as steel. It would have been impossible to have
told whether he was fifty or seventy. Eagerly
he smoothed out the abused missive and evidently succeeded even in the failing light, in
deciphering much of it, for the glimmer of a
smile flashed over his thin features as he thrust
the paper into his pocket.

Without a moment's hesitation he set out on
the trail of Captain Plum. A quarter of a mile

down the path he overtook the object of his pursuit.

"Ah, how do you do, sir?" he greeted as the younger man turned about upon hearing his approach. "A mighty fast pace you're setting for an old man, sir!" He broke into a laugh that was not altogether unpleasant, and boldly held out a hand. "We've been expecting you, but — not in this way. I hope there's nothing wrong?"

Captain Plum had accepted the proffered hand. Its coldness and the singular appearance of the old man who had come like an apparition chilled him. In a moment, however, it occurred to him that he was a victim of mistaken identity. As far as he knew there was no one on Beaver Island who was expecting him. To the best of his knowledge he was a fool for being there. His crew aboard the sloop had agreed upon that point with extreme vehemence and, to a man, had attempted to dissuade him from the mad project upon which he was launching himself

8

among the Mormons in their island stronghold. All this came to him while the little old man was looking up into his face, chuckling, and shaking his hand as if he were one of the most important and most greatly to be desired personages in the world.

" Hope there's nothing wrong, Cap'n? " he repeated.

" Right as a trivet here, Dad," replied the young man, dropping the cold hand that still persisted in clinging to his own. " But I guess you've got the wrong party. Who's expecting me? "

The old man's face wrinkled itself in a grimace and one gleaming eye opened and closed in an understanding wink.

" Ho, ho, ho! — of course you're not expected. Anyway, you're not *expected* to be expected! Cautious — a born general — mighty clever thing to do. Strang should appreciate it." The old man gave vent to his own approbation in a series of inimitable chuckles. " Is

9

that your sloop out there? " he inquired interestedly.

Something in the strangeness of the situation began to interest Captain Plum. He had planned a little adventure of his own, but here was one that promised to develop into something more exciting. He nodded his head.

" That's her."

" Splendid cargo," went on the old man. " Splendid cargo, eh? "

" Pretty fair."

" Powder in good shape, eh? "

" Dry as tinder."

" And balls — lots of balls, and a few guns, eh? "

" Yes, we *have* a few guns," said Captain Plum. The old man noted the emphasis, but the darkness that had fast settled about them hid the added meaning that passed in a curious look over the other's face.

" Odd way to come in, though — very odd! " continued the old man, gurgling and shaking as

10

if the thought of it occasioned him great merriment. "Very cautious. Level business head. Want to know that things are on the square, eh?"

"That's it!" exclaimed Captain Plum, catching at the proffered straw. Inwardly he was wondering when his feet would touch bottom. Thus far he had succeeded in getting but a single grip on the situation. Somebody was expected at Beaver Island with powder and balls and guns. Well, he had a certain quantity of these materials aboard his sloop, and if he could make an agreeable bargain —

The old man interrupted the plan that was slowly forming itself in Captain Plum's puzzled brain.

"It's the price, eh?" He laughed shrewdly. "You want to see the color of the gold before you land the goods. I'll show it to you. I'll pay you the whole sum to-night. Then you'll take the stuff where I tell you to. Eh? Isn't that so?" He darted ahead of Captain Plum with a quick alert movement. "Will you please follow me, sir?"

For an instant Captain Plum's impulse was to hold back. In that instant it suddenly occurred to him that he was lending himself to a rank imposition. At the same time he was filled with a desire to go deeper into the adventure, and his blood thrilled with the thought of what it might hold for him.

"Are you coming, sir?"

The little old man had stopped a dozen paces away and turned expectantly.

"I tell you again that you've got the wrong man, Dad!"

"Will you follow me, sir?"

"Well, if you'll have it so — damned if I won't!" cried Captain Plum. He felt that he had relieved his conscience, anyway. If things should develop badly for him during the next few hours no one could say that he had lied. So he followed light-heartedly after the old man, his eyes and ears alert, and his right hand, by force of habit, reaching under his coat to the butt of his pistol. His guide said not another word until they had traveled for half an hour along a twisting path and stood at last on the bald summit of a knoll from which they could look down upon a number of lights twinkling dimly a quarter of a mile away. One of these lights gleamed above all the others, like a beacon set among fireflies.

" That's St. James," said the old man. His voice had changed. It was low and soft, as though he feared to speak above a whisper.

" St. James ! "

The young man at his side gazed down silently upon the scattered lights, his heart throbbing in a sudden tumult of excitement. He had set out that day with the idea of resting his eyes on St. James. In its silent mystery the town now lay at his feet.

" And that light —" spoke the old man. He pointed a trembling arm toward the glare that shone more powerfully than the others. " That light marks the sacred home of the king!" His voice had again changed. A metallic hardness came into it, his words were vibrant with a strange excitement which he strove hard to conceal. It was still light enough for Captain Plum to see that the old man's black, beady eyes were startlingly alive with newly aroused emotion.

"You mean —"

"Strang!"

He started rapidly down the knoll and there floated back to Captain Plum the soft notes of his meaningless chuckle. A dozen rods farther on his mysterious guide turned into a by-path which led them to another knoll, capped by a good-sized building made of logs. There sounded the grating of a key in a lock, the shooting of a bolt, and a door opened to admit them.

"You will pardon me if I don't light up," apologized the old man as he led the way in. "A candle will be sufficient. You know there

14

must be privacy in these matters — always. Eh? Isn't that so?"

Captain Plum followed without reply. He guessed that the cabin was made up of one large room, and that at the present time, at least, it possessed no other occupant than the singular creature who had guided him to it.

"It is just as well, on this particular night, that no light is seen at the window," continued the old man as he rummaged about a table for a match and a candle. "I have a little corner back here that a candle will brighten up nicely and no one in the world will know it. Ho, ho, ho! — how nice it is to have a quiet little corner sometimes! Eh, Captain Plum?"

At the sound of his name Captain Plum started as though an unexpected hand had suddenly been laid upon him. So he *was* expected, after all, and his name was known! For a moment his surprise robbed him of the power of speech. The little old man had lighted his candle, and, grinning back over his shoulder,

passed through a narrow cut in the wall that
could hardly be called a door and planted his
light on a table that stood in the center of a
small room, or closet, not more than five feet
square. Then he coolly pulled Captain Plum's
old letter from his pocket and smoothed it out
in the dim light.

" Be seated, Captain Plum; right over there
— opposite me. So!"

He continued for a moment to smooth out the
creases in the letter and then proceeded to read
it with as much assurance as though its owner
were a thousand miles away instead of within
arm's reach of him. Captain Plum was dumfounded. He felt the hot blood rushing to his
face and his first impulse was to recover the
crumpled paper and demand something more
than an explanation. In the next instant it
occurred to him that this action would probably
spoil whatever possibilities his night's adventure
might have for him. So he held his peace.
The old man was so intent in his perusal of the

letter that the end of his hooked nose almost scraped the table. He went over the dim, partly obliterated words line by line, chuckling now and then, and apparently utterly oblivious of the other's presence. When he had come to the end he looked up, his eyes glittering with unbounded satisfaction, carefully folded the letter, and handed it to Captain Plum.

"That's the best introduction in the world, Captain Plum — the very best! Ho, ho! — it couldn't be better. I'm glad I found it." He chuckled gleefully, and rested his ogreish head in the palms of his skeleton-like hands, his elbows on the table. "So you're going back home — soon?"

"I haven't made up my mind yet, Dad," responded Captain Plum, pulling out his pipe and tobacco. "You've read the letter pretty carefully, I guess. What would you do?"

"Vermont?" questioned the old man shortly.

"That's it."

"Well, I'd go, and very soon, Captain Plum,

17

very soon, indeed: Yes, I'd hurry!" The old man jumped up with the quickness of a cat. So sudden was his movement that it startled Captain Plum, and he dropped his tobacco pouch. By the time he had recovered this article his strange companion was back in his seat again holding a leather bag in his hand. Quickly he untied the knot at its top and poured a torrent of glittering gold pieces out upon the table.

"Business — business and gold," he gurgled happily, rubbing his thin hands and twisting his fingers until they cracked. "A pretty sight, eh, Captain Plum? Now, to our account! A hundred carbines, eh? And a thousand of powder and a ton of balls. Or is it in lead? It doesn't make any difference — not a bit. It's three thousand, that's the account, eh?" He fell to counting rapidly.

For a full minute Captain Plum remained in stupefied bewilderment, silenced by the sudden and unexpected turn his adventure had taken. Fascinated, he watched the skeleton fingers as

18

they clinked the gold pieces. What was the mysterious plot into which he had allowed himself to be drawn? Why were a hundred guns and a ton and a half of powder and balls wanted by the Mormons of Beaver Island? Instinctively he reached out and closed his hand over the counting fingers of the old man. Their eyes met. And there was a shrewd, half-understanding gleam in the black orbs that fixed Captain Plum in an unflinching challenge. For a little space there was silence. It was Captain Plum who broke it.

" Dad, I'm going to tell you for the third and last time that you've made a mistake. I've got eight of the best rifles in America aboard my sloop out there. But there's a man for every gun. And I've got something hidden away underdeck that would blow up St. James in half an hour. And there is powder and ball for the whole outfit. But that's all. I'll sell you what I've got — for a good price. Beyond that you've got the wrong man!"

He settled back and blew a volume of smoke from his pipe. For another half minute the old man continued to look at him, his eyes twinkling, and then he fell to counting again.

Captain Plum was not given over to the habit of cursing. But now he jumped to his feet with an oath that jarred the table. The old man chuckled. The gold pieces clinked between his fingers. Coolly he shoved two glittering piles alongside the candle-stick, tumbled the rest back into the leather bag, deliberately tied the end, and smiled up into the face of the exasperated captain.

"To be sure you're not the man," he said, nodding his head until his elf-locks danced around his face. "Of course you're not the man. I know it — ho, ho! you can wager that I know it! A little ruse of mine, Captain Plum. Pardonable — excusable, eh? I wanted to know if you were a liar. I wanted to see if you were honest."

With a gasp of astonishment Captain Plum

20

Captain Plum

sank back into the chair. His jaw dropped and his pipe was held fireless in his hand.

" The devil you say! "

" Oh, certainly, certainly, if you wish it," chuckled the little man, in high humor. " I would have visited your sloop to-day, Captain Plum, if you hadn't come ashore so opportunely this morning. Ho, ho, ho! a good joke, eh? A mighty good joke! "

Captain Plum regained his composure by re-lighting his pipe. He heard the chink of gold pieces and when he looked again the two piles of money were close to the edge of his side of the table.

" That's for you, Captain Plum. There's just a thousand dollars in those two piles." There was tense earnestness now in the old man's face and voice. " I've imposed on you," he continued, speaking as one who had suddenly thrown off a disguise. " If it had been any other man it would have been the same. I want help. I want an honest man. I want a man whom I can trust. I will give you a thousand dollars if you will take a package back to your vessel with you and will promise to deliver it as quickly as you can."

"I'll do it!" cried Captain Plum. He jumped to his feet and held out his hand. But the old man slipped from his chair and darted swiftly out into the blackness of the adjoining room. As he came back Captain Plum could hear his insane chuckling.

"Business — business — business —" he gurgled. "Eh, Captain Plum? Did you ever take an oath?" He tossed a book on the table. It was the Bible.

Captain Plum understood. He reached for the book and held it under his left hand. His right he lifted above his head, while a smile played about his lips.

"I suppose you want to place me under oath to deliver that package," he said.

The old man nodded. His eyes gleamed with a feverish glare. A sudden hectic flush had gathered in his death-like cheeks. He trembled. His voice rose barely above a whisper.

"Repeat," he commanded. "I, Captain Nathaniel Plum, do solemnly swear before God ——"

A thrilling inspiration shot into Captain Plum's brain.

"Hold!" he cried. He lowered his hand. With something that was almost a snarl the old man sprang back, his hands clenched. "I will take this oath upon one other consideration," continued Captain Plum. "I came to Beaver Island to see something of the life and something of the people of St. James. If you, in turn, will swear to show me as much as you can to-night I will take the oath."

The old man was beside the table again in an instant.

"I will show it to you — all — all —" he exclaimed excitedly. "I will show it to you — yes, and swear to it upon the body of Christ!"

23

Captain Plum lifted his hand again and word by word repeated the oath. When it was done the other took his place.

" Your name? " asked Captain Plum.

A change scarcely perceptible swept over the old man's face.

" Obadiah Price."

" But you are a Mormon. You have the Bible there? "

Again the old man disappeared into the adjoining room. When he returned he placed two books side by side and stood them on edge so that he might clasp both between his bony fingers. One was the Bible, the other the Book of the Mormons. In a cracked, excited voice he repeated the strenuous oath improvised by Captain Plum.

" Now," said Captain Plum, distributing the gold pieces among his pockets, " I'll take that package."

This time the old man was gone for several minutes. When he returned he placed a small package tightly bound and sealed into his companion's hand.

" More precious than your life, more priceless than gold," he whispered tensely, " yet worthless to all but the one to whom it is to be delivered."

There were no marks on the package.

" And who is that? " asked Captain Plum.

The old man came so close that his breath fell hot upon the young man's cheek. He lifted a hand as though to ward sound from the very walls that closed them in.

" Franklin Pierce, President of the United States of America! "

CHAPTER II

THE SEVEN WIVES

HARDLY had the words fallen from the lips of Obadiah Price than the old man straightened himself and stood as rigid as a gargoyle, his gaze penetrating into the darkness of the room beyond Captain Plum, his head inclined slightly, every nerve in him strained to a tension of expectancy. His companion involuntarily gripped the butt of his pistol and faced the narrow entrance through which they had come. In the moment of absolute silence that followed there came to him, faintly, a sound, unintelligible at first, but growing in volume until he knew that it was the last echo of a tolling bell. There was no movement, no sound of breath or whisper from the old man at his back. But when it came again, floating to him as if from a vast distance, he turned quickly to find Obadiah Price with his face lifted, his thin arms flung wide above his head and his lips moving as if in prayer. His eyes burned with a dull glow as though he had been suddenly thrown into a trance. He seemed not to breathe, no vibration of life stirred him except in the movement of his lips. With the third toll of the distant bell he spoke, and to Captain Plum it was as if the passion and fire in his voice came from another being.

"Our Christ, Master of hosts, we call upon Thy chosen people the three blessings of the universe — peace, prosperity and plenty, and upon Strang, priest, king and prophet, the bounty of Thy power!"

Three times more the distant bell tolled forth its mysterious message and when the last echoes had died away the old man's arms dropped beside him and he turned again to Captain Plum.

"Franklin Pierce, President of the United States of America," he repeated, as though there had been no interruption since his companion's

27

question. " The package is to be delivered to him. Now you must excuse me. An important matter calls me out for a short time. But I will be back soon — oh, yes, very soon. And you will wait for me. You will wait for me here, and then I will take you to St. James."

He was gone in a quick hopping way, like a cricket, and the last that Captain Plum saw of him was his ghostly face turned back for an instant in the darkness of the next room, and after that the soft patter of his feet and the strange chuckle in his throat traveled to the outer door and died away as he passed out into the night. Nathaniel Plum was not a man to be easily startled, but there was something so unusual about the proceedings in which he was as yet playing a blind part that he forgot to smoke, which was saying much. Who was the old man? Was he mad? His eyes scanned the little room and an exclamation of astonishment fell from his lips when he saw the leather bag, partly filled with gold, lying where his mysterious acquaintance had dropped it. Surely this was madness or else another ruse to test his honesty. The discovery thrilled him. It was wonderfully quiet out in that next room and very dark. Were hidden eyes guarding that bag? Well, if so, he would give their owner to understand that he was not a thief. He rose from his chair and moved toward the bag, lifted it in his hand, and tossed it back again so that the gold in it chinked loudly. Then he went to the narrow aperture and blocked it with his body and listened until he knew that if there had been human life in the room he would have heard it.

The outer door was open and through it there came to him the soft breath of the night air and the sweetness of balsam and wild flowers. It struck him that it would be pleasanter waiting outside than in, and it would undoubtedly make no difference to Obadiah Price. In front of the cabin he found the stump of a log and seating himself on it where the clear light of the stars fell full upon him he once more began his interrupted smoke. It seemed to him that he had waited a long time when he heard the sound of footsteps. They came rapidly as if the person was half running. Hardly had he located the direction of the sound when a figure appeared in the opening and hurried toward the door of the cabin. A dozen yards from him it paused for a moment and turned partly about, as if inspecting the path over which it had come. With a greeting whistle Captain Plum jumped to his feet. He heard a little throat note, which was not the chuckling of Obadiah Price, and the figure ran almost into his arms. A sudden knowledge of having made a mistake drew Captain Plum a pace backward. For scarcely more than five seconds he found himself staring into the white terrified face of a girl. Eyes wide and glowing with sudden fright met his own. Instinctively he lifted his hand to his hat, but before he could speak the girl sprang back with a low cry and ran swiftly down the path that led into the gloom of the woods.

THE SEVEN WIVES

For several minutes Captain Plum stood as if the sudden apparition had petrified him. He listened long after the sound of retreating footsteps had died away. There remained behind a faint sweet odor of lilac which stirred his soul and set his blood tingling. It was a beautiful face that he had seen. He was sure of that and yet he could have given no good verbal proof of it. Only the eyes and the odor of lilac remained with him and after a little the lilac drifted away. Then he went back to the log and sat down. He smiled as he thought of the joke that he had unwittingly played on Obadiah. From his knowledge of the Beaver Island Mormons he was satisfied that the old man who displayed gold in such reckless profusion was anything but a bachelor. In all probability this was one of his wives and the cabin behind him, he concluded, was for some reason isolated from the harem. "Evidently that little Saintess is not a flirt," he concluded, "or she would have given me time to speak to her."

THE COURAGE OF CAPTAIN PLUM

The continued absence of Obadiah Price began to fill Captain Plum with impatience. After an hour's wait he reëntered the cabin and made his way to the little room, where the candle was still burning dimly. To his astonishment he beheld the old man sitting beside the table. His thin face was propped between his hands and his eyes were closed as if he was asleep. They shot open instantly on Captain Plum's appearance.

"I've been waiting for you, Nat," he cried, straightening himself with spring-like quickness. "Waiting for you a long time, Nat!" He rubbed his hands and chuckled at his own familiarity. "I saw you out there enjoying yourself. What did you think of her, Nat?" He winked with such audacious glee that, despite his own astonishment, Captain Plum burst into a laugh. Obadiah Price held up a warning hand. "Tut, tut, not so loud!" he admonished. His face was a map of wrinkles. His little black eyes shone with silent laughter.

There was no doubt but that he was immensely pleased over something. " Tell me, Nat — why did you come to St. James? "

He leaned forward over the table, his odd white head almost resting on it, and twiddled his thumbs with wonderful rapidity. " Eh, Nat? " he urged. " Why did you come? "

" Because it was too hot and uninteresting lying out there in a calm, Dad," replied the master of the *Typhoon*. " We've been roasting for thirty-six hours without a breath to fill our sails. I came over to see what you people are like. Any harm done? "

" Not a bit, not a bit — yet," chuckled the old man. " And what's your business, Nat? "

" Sailing — mostly."

" Ho, ho, ho! of course, I might have known it! Sailing — *mostly*. Why, certainly you sail! And why do you carry a pistol on one side of you and a knife on the other, Nat? "

" Troublous times, Dad. Some of the fisher-folk along the Northern End aren't very scrupulous. They took a cargo of canned stuffs from me a year back."

" And what use do you make of the four-pounder that's wrapped up in tarpaulin under your deck, Nat? And what in the world are you going to do with five barrels of gunpowder? "

" How in blazes —" began Captain Plum.

" O, to be sure, to be sure — they're for the fisher-folk," interrupted Obadiah Price. " Blow 'em up, eh, Nat? And you seem to be a young man of education, Nat. How did you happen to make a mistake in your count? Haven't you twelve men aboard your sloop instead of eight, Nat? Aren't there twelve instead of eight? Eh, Nat? "

" The devil take you! " cried Captain Plum, leaping suddenly to his feet, his face flaming red. " Yes, I have got twelve men and I've got a gun in tarpaulin and I've got five barrels of gunpowder! But how in the name of Kingdom-Come did you find it out? "

Obadiah Price came around the end of the table and stood so close to Captain Plum that a person ten feet away could not have heard him when he spoke.

" I know more than that, Nat," he whispered. " Listen! A little while ago — say two weeks back — you were becalmed off the head of Beaver Island, and one dark night you were boarded by two boat-loads of men who made you and your crew prisoners, robbed you of everything you had,— and the next day you went back to Chicago. Eh? "

Nathaniel stood speechless.

" And you made up your mind the pirates were Mormons, enlisted some of your friends, armed your ship — and you're back here to make us settle. Isn't it so, Nat? "

The little old man was rubbing his hands eagerly, excitedly.

" You tried to get the revenue cutter *Michigan* to come down with you, but they wouldn't — ho, ho, they wouldn't! One of our friends in Chicago sent quick word ahead of you to tell me all about it, and — Strang, the king, doesn't know!"

He spoke the last words in intense earnestness.

Then, suddenly, he held out his hand.

"Young man, will you shake hands with me? Will you shake hands? — and then we will go to St. James!"

Captain Plum thrust out a hand and the old man gripped it. The thin fingers tightened like cold clamps of steel. For a moment the face of Obadiah Price underwent a strange change. The hardness and glitter went out of his eyes and in place there came a questioning, almost an appealing, look. His tense mouth relaxed. It was as if he was on the point of surrendering to some emotion which he was struggling to stifle. And Nathaniel, meeting those eyes, felt that somewhere within him had been struck a strange chord of sympathy, something that made this little old man more than a half-

36

mad stranger to him, and involuntarily the grip of his fingers tightened around those of his companion.

"Now we will go to St. James, Captain Plum!"

He attempted to withdraw his hand but Captain Plum held to it.

"Not yet!" he exclaimed. "There are two or three things which your friend didn't tell you, Obadiah Price!"

Nathaniel's eyes glittered dangerously.

"When I left ship this morning I gave explicit orders to Casey, my mate."

He gazed steadily into the old man's unflinching eyes.

"I said something like this: 'Casey, I'm going to see Strang before I come back. If he's willing to settle for five thousand, we'll call it off. And if he isn't — why, we'll stand out there a mile and blow St. James into hell! And if I don't come back by to-morrow at sundown, Casey, you take command and blow it to hell without me!' So, Obadiah Price, if there's treachery—"

The old man clutched at his hands with insane fierceness.

"There will be no treachery, Nat, I swear to God there will be no treachery! Come, we will go—"

Still Captain Plum hesitated.

"Who are you? Whom am I to follow?"

"A member of our holy Council of Twelve, Nat, and lord high treasurer of His Majesty, King Strang!"

Before Captain Plum could recover from the surprise of this whispered announcement the little old man had freed himself and was pattering swiftly through the darkness of the next room. The master of the *Typhoon* followed close behind him. Outside the councilor hesitated for a moment, as if debating which route to take, and then with a prodigious wink at Captain Plum and a throatful of his inimitable chuckles, chose the path down which his startled visitor of a short time before had fled. For fifteen minutes this path led between thick black walls of forest verdure. Obadiah Price kept always a few paces ahead of his companion and spoke not a word. At the end of perhaps half a mile the path entered into a large clearing on the farther side of which Nathaniel caught the glimmer of a light. They passed close to this light, which came from the window of a large square house built of logs, and Captain Plum became suddenly conscious that the air was filled with the redolent perfume of lilac. With half a dozen quick strides he overtook the councilor and caught him by the arm.

" I smell lilac! " he exclaimed.

" Certainly, so do I," replied Obadiah Price. " We have very fine lilacs on the island."

" And I smelled lilac back there," continued Nathaniel, still holding to the old man's arm, and pointing a thumb over his shoulder. " I smelled 'em back there, when—"

" Ho, ho, ho ! " chuckled the councilor softly.

" I don't doubt it, Nat, I don't doubt it. She is very fond of lilacs. She wears the flowers very often."

He pulled himself away and Captain Plum could hear his queer chuckling for some time after. Soon they entered the gloom of the woods again and a little later came out into another clearing and Nathaniel knew that it was St. James that lay at his feet. The lights of a few fishing boats were twinkling in the harbor, but for the most part the town was dark. Here and there a window shone like a spot of phosphorescent yellow in the dismal gloom and the great beacon still burned steadily over the home of the prophet.

" Ah, it is not time," whispered Obadiah. " It is still too early." He drew his companion out of the path which they had followed and sat himself down on a hummock a dozen yards away from it, inviting Nathaniel by a pull of the sleeve to do the same. There were three of these hummocks, side by side, and Captain Plum

chose the one nearest the old man and waited
for him to speak. But the councilor did not
open his lips. Doubled over until his chin
rested almost upon the sharp points of his knees,
he gazed steadily at the beacon, and as he
looked it shuddered and grew dark, like a fire-
fly that suddenly closes its wings. With a
quick spring the councilor straightened himself
and turned to the master of the *Typhoon*.

" You have a good nose, Nat," he said, " but
your ears are not so good. Sh-h-h-h!" He
lifted a hand warningly and nodded sidewise
toward the path. Captain Plum listened. He
heard low voices and then footsteps — voices
that were approaching rapidly, and were those
of women, and footsteps that were almost running. The old man caught him by the arm and
as the sounds came nearer his grip tightened.

" Don't frighten them, Nat. Get down!"

He crouched until he was only a part of the
shadows of the ground and following his ex-
ample Nathaniel slipped between two of the

knolls. A few yards away the sound of the voices ceased and there was a hesitancy in the soft tread of the approaching steps. Slowly, and now in awesome silence, two figures came down the path and when they reached a point opposite the hummocks Nathaniel could see that they turned their faces toward them and that for a brief space there was something of terror in the gleam he caught of their eyes. In a moment they had passed. Then he heard them running.

"They saw us!" Captain Plum exclaimed.

Obadiah hopped to his feet and rubbed his hands with great glee. "What a temptation, Nat!" he whispered. "What a temptation to frighten them out of their wits! No, they didn't see us, Nat — they didn't see us. The girls are always frightened when they pass these graves. Some day—"

"Graves!" almost shouted the master of the *Typhoon*. "Graves — and we sitting on 'em!"

"That's all right, Nat — that's all right.

They're my graves, so we're welcome to sit on them. I often come here and sit for hours at a time. They like to have me, especially little Jean — the middle one. Perhaps I'll tell you about Jean before you go away."

If Captain Plum had been watching him he would have seen that soft mysterious light again shining in the old councilor's eyes. But now Nathaniel stood erect, his nostrils sniffing the air, catching once more the sweet scent of lilac. He hurried out into the opening, with the old man close behind him, and peered down into the starlit gloom into which the two girls had disappeared. The lovely face that had appeared to him for an instant at Obadiah's cabin began to haunt him. He was sure now that his sudden appearance had not been the only cause of its terror, and he felt that he should have called out to her or followed until he had overtaken her. He could easily have excused his boldness, even if the councilor had been watching him from the cabin door. He was certain that she had passed very near to him again and that the fright which Obadiah had attempted to explain was not because of the graves. He swung about upon his companion, determined to ask for an explanation. The latter seemed to divine his thought.

" Don't let a little scent of lilac disturb you so, young man," he said with singular coldness. "It may cause you great unpleasantness." He went ahead and Nathaniel followed him, assured that the old man's words and the way in which he had spoken them no longer left a doubt as to the identity of his night visitor. She was one of the councilor's wives, so he thought, and his own interest in her was beginning to have an irritating effect. In other words Obadiah was becoming jealous.

For some time there was silence between the two. Obadiah Price now walked with extreme slowness and along paths which seemed to bring him no nearer to the town below. Nathaniel could see that he was absorbed in thoughts of his own, and held his peace. Was it possible that he had spoiled his chances with the councilor because of a pretty face and a bunch of lilacs? The thought tickled Captain Plum despite the delicacy of his situation and he broke into an involuntary laugh. The laugh brought Obadiah to a halt as suddenly as though some one had thrust a bayonet against his breast.

"Nat, you've got good red blood in you," he cried, whirling about. "D'ye suppose you can hate as well as love?"

"Lord deliver us!" exclaimed the astonished Captain Plum. "Hate — love — what the —"

"Yes, *hate*," repeated the old man with fierce emphasis, so close that his breath struck Nathaniel's face. "You can love a pretty face — and you can *hate*. I know you can. If you couldn't I would send you back to your sloop with the package to-night. But as it is I am going to relieve you of your oath. Yes, Nat, I give you back your oath — for a time."

Nathaniel stepped a pace back and put his

hands on his pockets as if to protect the gold there.

"You mean that you want to call off our bargain?" he asked.

The councilor rubbed his hands until the friction of them sent a shiver up Nathaniel's back. "Not that, Nat — O, no, not that! The bargain is good. The gold is yours. You must deliver the package. But you need not do it immediately. Understand? I am lonely back there in my shack. I want company. You must stay with me a week. Eh? Lilacs and pretty faces, Nat! Ho, ho! — You will stay a week, won't you, Nat?"

He spoke so rapidly and his face underwent so many changes, now betraying the keenest excitement, now wrinkled in an ogreish, bantering grin, now almost pleading in its earnestness, that Nathaniel knew not what to make of him. He looked into the beady eyes, sparkling with passion, and the cat-like glitter of them set his blood tingling. What strange adventure was this old man dragging him into? What were the motives, the reasoning, the plot that lay behind this mysterious creature's apparent faith in him? He tried to answer these things in the passing of a moment before he replied. The councilor saw his hesitancy and smiled.

"I will show you many things of interest, Nat," he said. "I will show you just one to-night. Then you will make up your mind, eh? You need not tell me until then."

He took the lead again and this time struck straight down for the town. They passed a number of houses built of logs and Nathaniel caught narrow gleams of light from between close-drawn curtains. In one of these houses he heard the crying of children, and with a return of his grisly humor Obadiah Price prodded him in the ribs and said,

"Good old Israel Laeng lives there — two wives, one old, one young — eleven children. The Kingdom of Heaven is open to him!" And from a second he heard the sound of an organ,

and from still a third there came the laughter
and chatter of several feminine voices, and again
Obadiah reached out and prodded Nathaniel in
the ribs. There was one great, gloomy, long-
built place which they passed, without a ray of
light to give it life, and the councilor said,
" Three widows there, Nat,— fight like cats and
dogs. Poor Job killed himself." They avoided
the more thickly populated part of the settlement
and encountered few people, which seemed to
please the councilor. Once they overtook and
passed a group of women clad in short skirts and
loose waists and with their hair hanging in
braids down their backs. For a third time
Obadiah nudged Captain Plum.

" It is the king's pleasure that all women
wear skirts that come just below the knees," he
whispered. " Some of them won't do it and
he's wondering how to punish them. To-morrow there's going to be two public whippings.
One of the victims is a man who said that if he
was a woman he'd die before he put on knee

skirts. After he's whipped he is going to be made to wear 'em. By Urim and Thummin, isn't that choice, Nat?"

He shivered with quiet laughter and dived into a great block of darkness where there seemed to be no houses, keeping close beside Nathaniel. Soon they came to the edge of a grove and deep among the trees Captain Plum caught a glimpse of a lighted window. Obadiah Price now began to exhibit unusual caution. He approached the light slowly, pausing every few steps to peer guardedly about him, and when they had come very near to the window he pulled his companion behind a thick clump of shrubbery. Nathaniel could hear the old man's subdued chuckle and he bent his head to catch what he was about to whisper to him.

" You must make no noise, Nat," he warned. " This is the castle of our priest, king and prophet — James Jesse Strang. I am going to show you what you have never seen before and what you will never look upon again. I have sworn upon the Two Books and I will keep my oath. And then — you will answer the question I asked you back there."

He crept out into the darkness of the trees and Nathaniel followed, his heart throbbing with excitement, every sense alert, and one hand resting on the butt of his pistol. He felt that he was nearing the climax of his day's adventure and now, in the last moment of it, his old caution reasserted itself. He knew that he was among a dangerous people, men who, according to the laws of his country, were criminals in more ways than one. He had seen much of their work along the coasts and he had heard of more of it. He knew that this gloom and sullen quiet of St. James hid cut-throats and pirates and thieves. Still there was nothing ahead to alarm him. The old man dodged the gleams of the lighted window and slunk around to the end of the great house. Here, several feet above his head, was another window, small and veiled with the foliage of a vine that clung in dense masses to the log wall. With the assurance of one who had been there before the councilor mounted some object under the window, lifted himself until his chin was on a level with the glass, and peered within. He was there but an instant and then fell back, chuckling and rubbing his hands.

" Come, Nat! "

He stood a little to one side and bowed with mock politeness. For a moment Captain Plum hesitated. Under ordinary circumstances this spying through a window would have been repugnant to him. But at present something seemed to tell him that it was not to satisfy his curiosity alone that Obadiah Price had given him this opportunity. Would a look through that little window explain some of the mysteries of the night?

There came a low whisper in his ear.

" Do you smell lilac, Nat? Eh? "

The councilor was grinning at him. There was a suggestive gleam in his eyes. He rubbed his hands almost fiercely.

In another instant Captain Plum had stepped upon the object beneath the window and parted the leaves. Breathlessly he looked in. A strange scene met his eyes. He was looking into a vast room, illuminated by a huge hanging lamp suspended almost on a level with his head. Under this lamp there was a long table and at the table sat seven women and one man. The man was at the end nearest the window and all that Nat could see was the back of his head and shoulders. But the women were in full view, three on each side of the table and one at the far end. He guessed the man to be Strang; but he stared at the women and as his eyes traveled back to the one facing him at the end of the table he could scarcely repress the exclamation of surprise that rose to his lips. It was the girl whom he had encountered at the councilor's cabin. She was leaning forward as if in an agony of suspense, her eyes on the king, her lips parted, her hands clutching at a great book which lay open before her. Her cheeks were flushed with excitement. And even as he looked Captain Plum saw her head fall suddenly forward upon the table, encircled by her arms. The heavy braid of her hair, partly undone, glistened like red gold in the lamplight. Her slender body was convulsed with sobs. The woman nearest her reached over and laid a caressing hand on the bowed head, but drew it quickly away as if at a sharp command.

In his eagerness Nathaniel thrust his face through the foliage until his nose touched the glass. When the girl lifted her head she straightened back in her chair — and saw him. There came a sudden white fear in her face, a parting of the lips as if she were on the point of crying out, and then, before the others had seen, she looked again at Strang. She had discovered him and yet she had not revealed her discovery! Nathaniel could have shouted for joy. She had seen him, had recognized him! And because she had not cried out she wanted him! He drew his pistol from its holster and waited. If she signaled for him, if she called him, he would burst the window. The girl was talking now and as she talked she lifted her eyes. Nathaniel pressed his face close against the window, and smiled. That would let her know he was a friend. She seemed to answer him with a little nod and he fancied that her eyes glowed with a mute appeal for his assistance. But only for an instant, and then they turned again to the king. Not until that moment did Nathaniel notice upon her bosom a bunch of crumpled lilacs.

From below the iron grip of the councilor dragged him down.

" That's enough," he whispered. " That's enough — for to-night." He saw the pistol in Nathaniel's hand and gave a sudden breathless cry.

" Nat — Nat —"

He caught Captain Plum's free hand in his.

" Tell me this, Obadiah Price," whispered the master of the *Typhoon*, " who is she? "

THE SEVEN WIVES

The councilor stood on tiptoe to answer.

" They are the six wives of Strang, Nat! "

" But the other? " demanded Nathaniel.
" The other —

" O, to be sure, to be sure," chuckled Obadiah.
" The girl of the lilacs, eh? Why, she's the
seventh wife, Nat — that's all, the seventh
wife! "

CHAPTER III

So quickly that Obadiah Price might not have counted ten before it had come and gone the significance of his new situation flashed upon Captain Plum as he stood under the king's window. His plans had changed since leaving ship but now he realized that they had become hopelessly involved. He had intended that Obadiah should show him where Strang was to be found, and that later, when ostensibly returning to his vessel, he would visit the prophet in his home. Whatever the interview brought forth he would still be in a position to deliver the councilor's package. Even an hour's bombardment of St. James would not interfere with the fulfilment of his oath. But those few minutes at the king's win-

56

dow had been fatal to the scheme he had built. The girl had seen him. She had not betrayed his presence. She had called to him with her eyes — he would have staked his life on that. What did it all mean? He turned to Obadiah. The old man was grimacing and twisting his hands nervously. He seemed half afraid, cringing, as if fearing a blow. The sight of him set Nathaniel's blood afire. His white face seemed to verify the terrible thought that had leaped into his brain. Suddenly he heard a faint cry — a woman's voice — and in an instant he was back at the window. The girl had risen to her feet and stood facing him. This time, as her eyes met his own, he saw in them a flashing warning, and he obeyed it as if she had spoken to him. As he dropped silently back to the ground the councilor came close to his side.

"That's enough for to-night, Nat," he whispered.

He made as if to slip away but Nathaniel detained him with an emphatic hand.

" Not yet, Dad!   I'd like to have a word with
— this —"

" With Strang's wife," chuckled Obadiah.
" Ho, ho, ho, Nat, you're a rascal!"   The old
man's face was mapped with wrinkles, his eyes
glowed with joyous approbation.   " You shall,
Nat, you shall! You love a pretty face, eh?
You shall meet Mrs. Strang, Nat, and you shall
make love to her if you wish.   I swear that, too.
But not to-night, Nat — not to-night."

He stood a pace away and rubbed his hands.

" There will be no chance to-night, Nat —
but to-morrow night, or the next.   O, I promise you shall meet her, and make love to her, Nat!
Ho, if Strang knew, if Strang *only* knew!"

There was something so fiendishly gloating in
the councilor's attitude, in his face, in the hot
glow of his eyes, that for a moment Nathaniel's
involuntary liking for the little old man before
him turned to abhorrence.   The passion, the
triumph of the man, convinced him where words
had failed.   The girl was Strang's wife.   His

last doubt was dispelled. And because she was Strang's wife Obadiah hated the Mormon prophet. The councilor had spoken with fateful assurance — that he should meet her, that he should make love to her. It was an assurance that made him shudder. As he followed in silence up out of the gloom of the town he strove, but in vain, to find whether sin had lurked in the sweet face that had appealed to him in its misery — whether there had been a flash of something besides terror, besides prayerful entreaty, in the lovely eyes that had met his own. Obadiah spoke no word to break in on his thoughts. Now and then the old man's insane chucklings floated softly to Nathaniel's ears, and when at last they came to the cabin in the forest he broke into a low laugh that echoed weirdly in the great black room which they entered. He lighted another candle and approached a ladder which led through a trap in the ceiling. Without a word he mounted this ladder, and Nathaniel followed him, finding himself a moment later in a small low room furnished with a bed. The councilor placed his candle on a table close beside it and rubbed his hands until it seemed they must burn.

" You will stay — eh, Nat? " he cried, bobbing his head. " Yes, you will stay, and you will give me back the package for a day or two." He retreated to the trap and slid down it as quickly as a rat. " Pleasant dreams to you, Nat, and — O, wait a minute! " Captain Plum could hear him pattering quickly over the floor below. In a moment he was back, thrusting his white grimacing face through the trap and tossed something upon the bed. " She left them last night, Nat. Pleasant dreams, pleasant dreams," and he was gone.

Nathaniel turned to the bed and picked up a faded bunch of lilacs. Then he sat down, loaded his pipe, and smoked until he could hardly see the walls of his little room. From the moment of his landing on the island he turned the events of the day over in his mind. Yet when he arrived at the end of them he was no less mystified than when he began. Who was Obadiah Price? Who was the girl that fate had so mysteriously associated with his movements thus far? What was the plot in which he had accidentally become involved? With tireless tenacity he hung to these questions for hours. That there was a plot of some kind he had not the least doubt. The councilor's strange actions, the oath, the package, and above all the scene in the king's house convinced him of that. And he was sure that Obadiah's night visitor — the girl with the lilacs — was playing a vital part in it.

He plucked at the withered flowers which the old man had thrown him. He could detect their sweet scent above the pungent fumes of tobacco and as Obadiah's triumphant chuckle recurred to him, the gloating joy in his eyes, the passionate tremble of his voice, a grim smile passed over his face. The mystery was easy of solution — if he was willing to reason along certain lines. But he was not willing. He had formed his own picture of Strang's wife and it pleased him to keep it. At moments he half conceded himself a fool, but that did not trouble him. The longer he smoked the more his old confidence and his old recklessness returned to him. He had enjoyed his adventure. The next day he would end it. He would go openly into St. James and have done his business with Strang. Then he would return to his ship. What had he, Captain Plum, to do with Strang's wife?

But even after he had determined on these things his brain refused to rest. He paced back and forth across the narrow room, thinking of the man whom he was to meet to-morrow — of Strang, the one-time schoolmaster and temperance lecturer who had made himself a king, who for seven years had defied the state and nation, and who had made of his island stronghold a hot-bed of polygamy, of licentiousness, of dissolute power. His blood grew hot as he thought again of the beautiful girl who had appealed to

him.   Obadiah had said that she was the king's
wife.   Still —

Thoughts flashed into his head which for a
time made him forget his mission on the island.
In spite of his resolution to keep to his own
scheme he found himself, after a little, thinking
only of the Mormon king, and the lovely face he
had seen through the castle window.   He knew
much about the man with whom he was to deal
to-morrow.   He knew that he had been a rival
of Brigham Young and that when the exodus of
the Mormons to the deserts of the west came he
had led his own followers into the North, and
that each July, amid barbaric festivities, he was
recrowned with a circlet of gold.   But the girl!
If she was the king's wife why had her eyes
called to him for help?

The question crowded Nathaniel's brain with a
hundred thrilling pictures.   With a shudder he
thought of the terrible power the Mormon king
held not only over his own people but over the
Gentiles of the mainlands as well.   With these

mainlanders, he regarded Beaver Island as a nest of pirates and murderers. He knew of the depredations of Strang and his people among the fishermen and settlers, of the piratical expeditions of his armed boats, of the dreaded raids of his sheriffs, and of the crimes that made the women of the shores tremble and turn white at the mere mention of his name.

Was it possible that this girl —

Captain Plum did not let himself finish the thought. With a powerful effort he brought himself back to his own business on the island, smoked another pipe, and undressed. He went to bed with the withered lilacs on the table close beside him. He fell asleep with their scent in his nostrils. When he awoke they were gone. He started up in astonishment when he saw what had taken their place. Obadiah had visited him while he slept. The table was spread with a white cloth and upon it was his breakfast, a pot of coffee still steaming, and the whole of a cold baked fowl. Near-by, upon a chair, was a basin

of water, soap and a towel. Nathaniel rolled
from his bed with a healthy laugh of pleasure.
The councilor was at least a courteous host,
and his liking for the curious old man promptly
increased. There was a sheet of paper on his
plate upon which Obadiah had scribbled the following words:

"My dear Nat: — Make yourself at home.
I will be away to-day but will see you again to-
night. Don't be surprised if somebody makes
you a visit."

The "somebody" was heavily underscored
and Nathaniel's pulse quickened and a sudden
flush of excitement surged into his face as he
read the meaning of it. The "somebody" was
Strang's wife. There could be no other inter-
pretation. He went to the trap and called down
for Obadiah but there was no answer. The
councilor had already gone. Quickly eating
his breakfast the master of the *Typhoon* climbed
down the ladder into the room below. The re-

mains of the councilor's breakfast were on a table near the door, and the door was open. Through it came a glory of sunshine and the fresh breath of the forest laden with the perfume of wild flowers and balsam. A thousand birds seemed caroling and twittering in the sunlit solitude about the cabin. Beyond this there was no other sound or sign of life. For many minutes Nathaniel stood in the open, his eyes on the path along which he knew that Strang's wife would come — if she came at all. Suddenly he began to examine the ground where the girl had stood the previous night. The dainty imprints of her feet were plainly discernible in the soft earth. Then he went to the path — and with a laugh so loud that it startled the birds into silence he set off with long strides in the direction of St. James. From the footprints in that path it was quite evident that Strang's wife was a frequent visitor at Obadiah's.

At the edge of the forest, from where he could see the log house situated across the opening,

Nathaniel paused. He had made up his mind
that the girl whom he had seen through the
king's window was in some way associated with
it. Obadiah had hinted as much and she had
come from there on her way to Strang's. But
as the prophet's wives lived in his castle at St.
James this surely could not be her home. More
than ever he was puzzled. As he looked he saw
a figure suddenly appear from among the mass
of lilac bushes that almost concealed the cabin.
An involuntary exclamation of satisfaction escaped him and he drew back deeper among the
trees. It was the councilor who had shown himself. For a few moments the old man stood
gazing in the direction of St. James as if watching for the approach of other persons. Then
he dodged cautiously along the edge of the
bushes, keeping half within their cover, and
moved swiftly in the opposite direction toward
the center of the island. Nathaniel's blood
leaped with a desire to follow. The night before
he had guessed that Obadiah with his gold and

his smoldering passion was not a man to isolate himself in the heart of the forest. Here — across the open — was evidence of another side of his life. In that great square-built domicile of logs, screened so perfectly by flowering lilac, lived Obadiah's wives. Captain Plum laughed aloud and beat the bowl of his pipe on the tree beside him. And the *girl* lived there — or came from there to the woodland cabin so frequently that her feet had beaten a well-worn path. Had the councilor lied to him? Was the girl he had seen through the King's window one of the seven wives of Strang — or was she the wife of Obadiah Price?

The thought was one that thrilled him. If the girl was the councilor's wife what was the motive of Obadiah's falsehood? And if she was Strang's wife why had her feet — and hers alone with the exception of the old man's — worn this path from the lilac smothered house to the cabin in the woods? The captain of the *Typhoon* regretted now that he had given such explicit orders to Casey. Otherwise he would have followed the figure that was already disappearing into the forest on the opposite side of the clearing. But now he must see Strang. There might be delay, necessary delay, and if it so happened that his own blundering curiosity kept him on the island until sundown — well, he smiled as he thought of what Casey would do.

Refilling his pipe and leaving a trail of smoke behind him he set out boldly for St. James. When he came to the three graves he stopped, remembering that Obadiah had said they were his graves. A sort of grim horror began to stir at his soul as he gazed on the grass-grown mounds — proofs that the old councilor would inherit a place in the Mormon Heaven having obeyed the injunctions of his prophet on earth. Nathaniel now understood the meaning of his words of the night before. This was the family burying ground of the old councilor.

He walked on, trying in vain to concentrate his mind solely upon the business that was ahead of him. A few days before he would have counted this walk to St. James one of the events of his life. Now it had lost its fascination. Despite his efforts to destroy the vision of the beautiful face that had looked at him through the king's window its memory still haunted him. The eyes, soft with appeal; the red mouth, quivering, and with lips parted as if about to speak to him; the bowed head with its tumbled glory of hair — all had burned themselves upon his soul in a picture too deep to be eradicated. If St. James was interesting now it was because that face was a part of it, because the secret of its life, of the misery that it had confessed to him, was hidden somewhere down there among its scattered log homes.

Slowly he made his way down the slope in the direction of Strang's castle, the tower of which, surmounted by its great beacon, glistened in the morning sun. He would find Strang there. And there would be one chance in a thousand of seeing the girl — if Obadiah had spoken the truth. As he passed down he met men and boys coming up the slope and others moving along at the bottom of it, all going toward the interior of the island. They had shovels or rakes or hoes upon their shoulders and he guessed that the Mormon fields were in that direction; others bore axes; and now and then wagons, many of them drawn by oxen, left the town over the road that ran near the shore of the lake. Those whom he met stared at him curiously, much interested evidently in the appearance of a stranger. Nathaniel paid but small heed to them. As he entered the grove through which the councilor had guided him the night before his eagerness became almost excitement. He approached the great log house swiftly but cautiously, keeping as much from view as possible. As he came under the window through which he had looked upon the king and his wives his heart leaped with anticipation, with hope that was strangely mingled with fear. For only a moment he paused to listen, and notwithstanding the seriousness of his position he could not repress a smile as there came to his ears the crying of children and the high angry voice of a woman. He passed around to the front of the house. The door of Strang's castle was wide open and unguarded. No one had seen his approach; no one accosted him as he mounted the low steps; there was no one in the room into which he gazed a moment later. It was the great hall into which he had spied a few hours previous. There was the long table with the big book on it, the lamp whose light had bathed the girl's head in a halo of glory, the very chair in which he had found her sitting! He was conscious of a throbbing in his breast, a longing to call out — if he only knew her name.

In the room there were four closed doors and it was from beyond these that there came to him the wailing of children. A fifth door was open and through it he saw a cradle gently rocking. Here at last was visible life, or motion at least, and he knocked loudly. Very gradually the cradle ceased its movement. Then it stopped, and a woman came out into the larger room. In a moment Nathaniel recognized her as the one who had placed a caressing hand upon the bowed head of the sobbing girl the night before. Her face was of pathetic beauty. Its whiteness was startling. Her eyes shone with an unhealthy luster, and her dark hair, falling in heavy curls over her shoulder, added to the wonderful pallor of her cheeks.

Nathaniel bowed. " I beg your pardon, madam; I came to see Mr. Strang," he said.

" You will find the king at his office," she replied.

The woman's voice was low, but so sweet that it was like music to the ear. As she spoke she came nearer and a faint flush appeared in the transparency of her cheek.

" Why do you wish to see the king? " she asked.

Was there a tremble of fear in her voice? Even as he looked Nathaniel saw the flush deepen in her cheeks and her eyes light with nervous eagerness.

"I am sent by Obadiah Price," he hazarded.

A flash of relief shot into the woman's face.

"The king is at his office," she repeated. "His office is near the temple."

Nathaniel retired with another bow.

"By thunder, Strang, old boy, you've certainly got an eye for beauty!" he laughed as he hurried through the grove.

"And Obadiah Price must be somebody, after all!"

The Mormon temple was the largest structure in St. James, a huge square building of hewn logs, and Nathaniel did not need to make inquiry to find it. On one side was a two-story building with an outside stairway leading to the upper floor, and a painted sign announced that on this second floor was situated the office of James Jesse Strang, priest, king and prophet of the Mormons. It was still very early and the general merchandise store below was not open. Congratulating himself on this fact, and with the fingers of his right hand reaching instinctively for his pistol butt, Captain Plum mounted the stair. When half way up he heard voices. As he reached the landing at the top he caught the quick swish of a skirt. Another step and he was in the open door. He was not soon enough to see the person who had just disappeared through an opposite door but he knew that it was a woman. Directly in front of him as if she had been expecting his arrival was a young girl, and no sooner had he put a foot over the threshold than she hurried toward him, the most acute anxiety and fear written in her face.

"You are Captain Plum?" she asked breathlessly.

Nathaniel stopped in astonishment.

"Yes, I'm —"

"Then you must hurry — hurry!" cried the girl excitedly. "You have not a moment to lose! Go back to your ship before it is too late! She says they will kill you —"

"Who says so?" thundered Captain Plum. He sprang to the girl's side and caught her by the arm. "Who says that I will be killed? Tell me — who gave you this warning for me?"

"I — I — tell you so!" stammered the young girl. "I — I — heard the king — they will kill you —" Her lips trembled. Nathaniel saw that her eyes were already red from crying. "You will go?" she pleaded.

Nathaniel had taken her hand and now he held it tightly in his own. His head was thrown back, his eyes were upon the door across the room. When he looked again into the girlish face there was flashing joyous defiance in his eyes, and in his voice there was confession of the truth that had suddenly come to overwhelm whatever law of self preservation he might have held unto himself.

"No, my dear, I am not going back to my ship," he spoke softly. "Not unless she who is in that room comes out and bids me go herself!"

CHAPTER IV

THE WHIPPING

SCARCE had the words fallen from his lips when there sounded a slow, heavy step on the stair outside. The young girl snatched her hand free and caught Nathaniel by the wrist.

" It is the king! " she whispered excitedly. " It is the king! Quick — you still have time! You must go — you must go — "

She strove to pull him across the room.

" There — through that door! " she urged.

The slowly ascending steps were half way up the stairs. Nathaniel hesitated. He knew that a moment before there had passed through that door one who carried with her the odor of lilac and his heart leaped to its own conclusion who that person was. He had heard the rustle of the girl's skirt. He had seen the last inch of the

77

door close as Strang's wife pulled it after her. And now he was implored to follow! He sprang forward as the heavy steps neared the landing. His hand was upon the latch — when he paused. Then he turned and bent his head close down to the girl.

"No, I won't do it, my dear," he whispered. "Just now it might make trouble for — her."

He lifted his eyes and saw a man looking at him from the doorway. He needed no further proof to assure him that this was Strang the king of the Mormons, for the Beaver Island prophet was painted well in that region which knew the grip and terror of his power. He was a massive man, with the slow slumbering strength of a beast. He was not much under fifty; but his thick beard, reddish and crinkling, his shaggy hair, and the full-fed ruddiness of his face, with its foundation of heavy jaw, gave him a more youthful appearance. There was in his eyes, set deep and so light that they shone like pale blue glass, the staring assurance that is frequently born of power. In his hand he carried a huge metal-knobbed stick.

In an instant Nathaniel had recovered himself. He advanced a step, bowing coolly.

"I am Captain Plum, of the sloop *Typhoon*," he said. "I called at your home a short time ago and was directed to your office. As a stranger on the island I did not know that you had an office or I would have come here first."

"Ah!"

The king drew his right foot back half a pace and bowed so low that Nathaniel saw only the crown of his hat. When he raised his head the aggressive stare had gone out of his eyes and a welcoming smile lighted up his face as he advanced with extended hand.

"I am glad to see you, Captain Plum."

His voice was deep and rich, filled with that wonderful vibratory power which seems to strike and attune the hidden chords of one's soul. The man's appearance had not prepossessed Nathaniel, but at the sound of his voice he recognized that which had made him the prophet of men. As the warm hand of the king clasped his own Captain Plum knew that he was in the presence of a master of human destinies, a man whose ponderous red-visaged body was simply the crude instrument through which spoke the marvelous spirit that had enslaved thousands to him, that had enthralled a state legislature and that had hypnotized a federal jury into giving him back his freedom when evidence smothered him in crime. He felt himself sinking in the presence of this man and struggled fiercely to regain himself. He withdrew his hand and straightened himself like a soldier.

"I have come to you with a grievance, Mr. Strang," he began. "A grievance which I feel sure you will do your best to right. Perhaps you are aware that some little time ago — about two weeks back — your people boarded my ship in force and robbed me of several thousand dollars' worth of merchandise."

Strang had drawn a step back.

"Aware of it!" he exclaimed in a voice that shook the room. "Aware of it!" The red of his face turned purple and he clenched his free hand in sudden passion. "Aware of it!" He repeated the words, this time so gently that Nathaniel could scarcely hear them, and tapped his heavy stick upon the floor. "No, Captain Plum, I was not aware of it. If I *had* been —" He shrugged his thick shoulders. The movement, and a sudden gleam of his teeth through his beard, were expressive enough for Nathaniel to understand.

Then the king smiled.

"Are you sure — are you *quite* sure, Captain Plum, that it was my people who attacked your ship? If so, of course you must have some proof?"

"We were very near to Beaver Island and many miles from the mainland," said Nathaniel. "It could only have been your people."

"Ah!"

Strang led the way to a table at the farther

end of the room and motioned Nathaniel to a seat opposite him.

" We are a much persecuted people, Captain Plum, very much persecuted indeed." His wonderful voice trembled with a subdued pathos. " We have answered for many sins that have never been ours, Captain Plum, and among them are robbery, piracy and even murder. The people along the coasts are deadly enemies to us — who would be their friends; they commit crimes in our name and we do not retaliate. It was not my people who waylaid your vessel. They were fishermen, probably, who came from the Michigan shore and awaited their opportunity off Beaver Island. But I shall investigate this; believe me, I shall investigate this fully, Captain Plum!"

Nathaniel felt something like a great choking fist shoot up into his throat. It was not a sensation of fear but of humiliation — the humiliation of defeat, the knowledge of his own weakness in the hands of this man who had so quickly and so surely blocked his claim. His quick brain saw the futility of argument. He possessed no absolute proof and he had thought that he needed none. Strang saw the flash of doubt in his face, the hesitancy in his answer; he divined the working of the other's brain and in his soft voice, purring with friendship, he followed up his triumph.

"I sympathize with you," he spoke gently, "and my sympathy and word shall help you. We do not welcome strangers among us, for strangers have usually proved themselves our enemies and have done us wrong. But to you I give the freedom of our kingdom. Search where you will, at what hours you will, and when you have found a single proof that your stolen property is among my people — when you have seen a face that you recognize as one of the robbers, return to me and I shall make restitution and punish the evil-doers."

So intensely he spoke, so filled with reason and truth were his words, that Nathaniel thrust out his hand in token of acceptance of the king's terms. And as Strang gripped that hand Captain Plum saw the young girl's face over the prophet's shoulder — a face, white as death in its terror, that told him all he had heard was a lie.

"And when you have done with my people," continued the king, "you will go among that other race, along the mainland, where men have thrown off the restraints of society to give loose reign to lust and avarice; where the Indian is brutified that his wife may be intoxicated by compulsion and prostituted by violence before his eyes; where the forest cabins and the streets of towns are filled with half-breeds; where there stalk wretches with withered and tearless eyes, who are in nowise troubled by recollection of robbery, rape and murder. And *there* you will find whom you are looking for!"

Strang had risen to his feet. His eyes blazed with the fire of smothered hatred and passion and his great voice rolled through his beard, tremulous with excitement, but still deep and rich, like the booming of some melodious instrument. He flung aside his hat as he paced back and forth; his shaggy hair fell upon his shoulders; huge veins stood out upon his forehead — and Nathaniel sat mute as he watched this lion of a man whose great throat quivered with the power that might have stirred a nation — that might have made him president instead of king. He waited for the thunder of that throat and his nerves keyed themselves to meet its bursting passion. But when Strang spoke again it was in a voice as soft and as gentle as a woman's.

"Those are the men who have vilified us, Captain Plum; who have covered us with crimes that we have never committed; who have driven our people into groups that they may be free from depredation; who watch like vultures to despoil our women; wild wifeless men, Captain Plum, who have left families and character behind them and who have sought the wilderness to escape the penalties of law and order. It is they who would destroy us. Go among my own people first, Captain Plum, and find your lost property if you can; and if you can not discover it where in seven years not one child has been born out of wedlock, seek among the Lamanites —— and my sheriffs shall follow where you place the crime!"

He had stretched out his arms like one whose plea was of life and death; his face shone with earnestness; his low words throbbed as if his heart were borne upon them for the inspection of its truth and honor. He was Strang the tragedian, the orator, the conqueror of a legislature, a governor, a dozen juries — and of human souls. And as he stood silent for a moment in this attitude Nathaniel rose to his feet, subservient, and believing as others had believed in the fitness of this man. But as his eyes traveled a dozen paces beyond, he saw the young girl gesturing to him in that same terror, and holding up for him to see a slip of paper upon which she had written. And when she had caught his eyes she crumpled the paper into a shapeless ball and tossed it just over the landing to the ground below the stair.

"'I thank you for the privileges of the island which you have offered me," said Nathaniel, putting on his hat, " and I shall certainly take advantage of your kindness for a few hours, as I want very much to witness one of your ceremonies which I understand is to take place to-day. Then, if I have discovered nothing, I shall return to my ship."

" Ah, you wish to see the whipping?" The king smiled his approval. " That is one way we have of punishing slight misdemeanors in our kingdom, Captain Plum. It is an illustration of our intolerance of evil-doers." He turned suddenly toward the girl. " Winnsome, my dear, have you copied the paper I was at work on? I wish to show it to Captain Plum."

He walked slowly toward her and for the first time since her warning Nathaniel had an opportunity of observing the girl without fear of being perceived by the prophet. She was very young, hardly more than a child he would have guessed at first; and yet at a second and more careful glance he knew that she could not be under fifteen — perhaps sixteen. Her whole attire was one to add to her childish appearance. Her hair, which was rather short, fell in lustrous dark curls about her face and upon her neck. She wore a fitted coat-like blouse, and knee skirts which disclosed a pretty pair of legs and ankles. As Strang was returning with the paper which she handed to him the girl turned her face to Captain Plum. Her mouth was formed into a round red O and she pointed anxiously to where she had thrown the note. The king's eyes were on his paper and Nathaniel nodded to assure her that he understood.

"I am like a gardener who compels every passing neighbor to go into his back yard and admire his first sprouts," laughed the prophet jovially. "In other words, I do a little writing, and I take a kind of childish joy in making other people read it. But I see this is not in proper shape, so you have escaped. It is a brief history of Beaver Island written at the request of the Smithsonian Institute, which has already published an article of mine. If you happen to be on the island to-morrow and should you return to this office I shall certainly have you read it if I have to call all of my sheriffs into service!"

He laughed with such open good-humor that Nathaniel found himself smiling despite the varied unpleasant sensations within him. "Do you write much?" he asked.

"I get out a daily paper," said the king rather proudly, "and of course, as prophet, I am the translator of what word may be handed down to us from Heaven for the direction and commandment of my people. I hold the secret of the Urim and Thummin, which was first delivered by angels into the hands of Joseph, and with it have revealed the word of God as it appears in a book which I have written. Ah —

I had forgotten this!" From among a mass of papers and books on the table he drew forth a blue-covered pamphlet and passed it to his companion. "I have only a few copies left but you may have this one, Captain Plum. It will surely interest you. In it I have set forth the troubles existing between my own people and the cyprian-rotted criminals that infest Mackinac and the mainland and have described our struggle for chastity and honor against these human vultures. It was published two years ago. But conditions are different to-day. Now — now I am king, and the oppressors in the filth of their crime have become the oppressed!"

The last words boomed from him in a slogan of triumph and as if in echoing mockery there came from the open door the chuckling, mirthless laugh of Obadiah Price.

"Yea — yea — even into the land of the Lamanites are you king!"

At the sound of his voice Strang turned toward him and the sonorous triumph that rumbled in his throat faded to a low greeting. And Nathaniel saw that the little old councilor's eyes glittered boldly as they met the prophet's and that in their glance was neither fear nor servitude but rather a light as of master meeting master. The two advanced and clasped hands and a few low words passed between them while Nathaniel went to the door.

"I will go with you, Captain Nathaniel Plum," called Obadiah. "I will go with you and show you the town."

"The councilor will be your friend," added Strang. "To-day he carries with him that authority from the king."

He bowed and Nathaniel passed through the door. Looking back he caught a last warning flash from the girl's eyes. As he hurried down the stair he heard the councilor pause for an instant upon the landing and taking advantage of this opportunity he picked up the bit of crumpled paper, and read these lines:

"Hurry to your ship. In another hour men will be watching for an opportunity to kill you. You will never leave the island alive — *unless you go now.* The girl you saw through the window sends you this warning."

He thrust the paper into his coat pocket as Obadiah came up behind him.

"Ho, ho, Nat, my boy, I have come fast to catch you — I have come fast!" he whispered. He caught his companion by the arm and Nathaniel felt his hand trembling violently. "Come this way, Nat — beyond the temple. I have things to say to you." His voice was strangely unnatural and when Captain Plum looked down into his face the look in the bead-like eyes startled him. "Nat, you must hurry away with the package!"

"So I understand — if I save my skin. Obadiah Price, I have a notion to kill you!"

They had passed beyond the huge edifice of logs, and as he stopped, hidden from the view of the king's office, Nathaniel caught the councilor's arm in a grip that crushed to the bone.

" I have a notion to kill you! " he repeated.

The old man stood unflinching. Not a muscle of his face quivered as the captain's fingers sank into his flesh.

" At the first sign of treachery, at the first sign of danger to myself, I shall shoot you dead! " he finished.

" You may, Nat, you may. From this moment until you leave the island I shall be at your side and no harm shall come to you. But if there should, Nat, or if there should come a moment when you believe that I am your enemy — shoot me! " There was sincerity in his voice that carried conviction to Nathaniel's heart and he released his hold upon the councilor's arm. Regardless of the mystery that surrounded him he believed in Obadiah. But there rose in his breast a mad desire to choke this old man into telling him the truth, to force him to reveal the secrets of this strange plot into which he had been drawn and of which he knew as little as when he first set foot in Strang's kingdom. Yet he realized even as the desire formed itself in his brain that such an effort would be useless.

"If you had remained at the cabin, Nat, you would have known that I was your friend," continued Obadiah. "She would have come to you, but now — it is impossible. You know. You have been warned?"

Nathaniel drew Winnsome's note from his pocket and read it aloud. Obadiah smiled gleefully when he noticed how carefully he kept the handwriting from his eyes.

"Ah, Nat, you are a noble fellow!" he cried, rubbing his hands in his old tireless way. "You would not betray pretty little Winn, eh? And who do you suppose told Winnsome to give you this note?"

"Strang's wife."

"Yea, even so. And it was she who set my old legs a-running for you, my boy. Come, let us move!"

The little councilor was his old self again, chuckling and grimacing and rubbing his hands, and his eyes danced as he spoke of the girl.

" Casey is not a cautious man," he gurgled with a sudden upward leer. " Casey is a fool!"

" Casey!" almost shouted Captain Plum. " What the devil do you mean? "

" Ho, ho, ho — haven't you guessed the truth yet, Nat? While you and I were getting acquainted last night a couple of fishermen from the mainland dropped alongside your sloop. They had been robbed by the Mormon pirates! They cursed Strang. They swore vengeance. And your cautious Casey cursed with 'em, and fed 'em, and drank with 'em — and he would have had them stay until morning only they were anxious to hurry with their report to Strang. Understand, Nat? Eh? Do you understand? "

" What did Casey tell them? " gasped Nathaniel.

Obadiah hunched his shoulders.

" Enough to warrant a bullet through your head, Nat. Cheerful, isn't it? But we'll fool them, Nat, we'll fool them! You shall board your ship and hurry away with the package, and then you shall make love to Strang's wife — *for she will go with you!* "

He stopped to enjoy the amazement that was written in every lineament of the other's face. The red blood surged into Nathaniel's neck and deepened on his bronze cheeks. Slowly the reaction came. When he spoke there was an uneasy gleam in his eyes and his voice was as hard as steel.

" She will go with me, Councilor! And why? "

Obadiah had laughed softly as he watched the change. Suddenly he jerked himself erect.

" Sh-h-h! " he whispered. " Keep cool, Nat! Don't show any excitement or fear. Here comes the man who is to kill you! "

He made no move save with his eyes.

"He is coming to speak with me and to get a good look at you," he added in excited haste. "Appear friendly. Agree with what I say. He is the chief of sheriffs, the king's murderer — Arbor Croche!"

He turned as if he had just seen the approaching figure. And he whispered softly, "Winnsome's father!"

Arbor Croche! Nathaniel gave an involuntary shudder as he turned with Obadiah. Croche, chief of sheriffs, scourge of the mainland — the Attila of the Mormon kingdom, whose very name caused the women of the shores to turn white and on whose head the men had secretly set a price in gold! Without knowing it his hand went under his coat. Obadiah saw the movement and as he advanced to meet the officer of the king he jerked the arm back fiercely. Half a dozen paces away the chief of sheriffs paused and bowed low. But the councilor stood erect, as he had stood before the king, smiling and nodding his head.

"Ah, Croche," he greeted, "good morning!"

"Good morning, Councilor!"

"Sheriff, I would have you meet Captain Nathaniel Plum, master of the sloop *Typhoon*. Captain Plum this is His Majesty's officer, Arbor Croche!"

The two men advanced and shook hands. Nathaniel stood half a head above the sheriff, who, like his master, the king, was short and of massive build, though a much younger man. He was a dark lowering hulk of a creature, with black eyes, black hair, and a hand-clasp that showed him possessed of great strength.

"You are a stranger, Captain Plum?"

The councilor replied quickly.

"He has never been at St. James before, sheriff. I have invited him to stay over to see the whipping. By the way —" he shot a suggestive look at the officer. "By the way, Croche, I want you to see him safely aboard his sloop to-night. His ship is at the lower end of the island, and if you will detail a couple of men just before dusk — an escort, you know —"

Nathaniel felt a curious thrill creep up his spine at the satisfaction which betrayed itself in the officer's black face.

" It will give me great pleasure, Councilor," he interrupted. " I shall escort you myself if you will allow me, Captain Plum! "

" Thank you," said Nathaniel.

" Captain Plum is to remain with me throughout the day," added Obadiah. " Come at seven — to my place. Ah, I see that people are assembling near the jail! "

" We have changed our plans somewhat, Councilor." The officer turned to Nathaniel. " You will see the whipping within half an hour, Captain Plum." He turned away with another bow to the councilor and hastened in the direction of Strang's office.

" So that is the gentleman who thinks he is going to put a bullet through me! " exclaimed Nathaniel when the officer had gone beyond hearing. He laughed, and there was a kind of wild expectant joy in his voice. "Obadiah, can you not make arrangements for him to go with me alone?"

"He will not go with you at all, Nat," gloated the old man. "Ho, ho, we are playing at his own game — treachery. When he calls at my place you will be aboard ship."

"But I should like to have a talk with him — alone, and in the woods. God — I know a man at Grand Traverse Bay whose wife and daughter —"

"Sh-h-h-h!" interrupted the councilor. "Would you kill little Winnsome's father?"

"Her father? That animal! That murderer! Is it true?"

"But you should have seen her mother, Nat, you should have seen her mother!" The old man twisted his hands, like a miser ravished by the sight of gold. "She was beautiful — as beautiful as a wild flower, and she killed herself three years ago to save the birth of another child into this hell. Little Winn is like her mother, Nat."

" And she lives with him? "

" Er, yes — and guarded, oh, so carefully guarded by Strang, Nat! Yes, I guess that some day she will be a queen."

" Great God!" cried the young man. " And you — you live in this cesspool of sin and still believe in a Heaven? "

" Yes, I believe in a Heaven. And my reward there shall be great. Ho, ho, I am taking no middle road, Nat! "

They had passed in a semicircle beyond the temple and now approached a squat building constructed of logs, which Obadiah had pointed out as the jail. A glance satisfied Nathaniel that it was so situated that an admirable view of the proceedings could be obtained from the rear of the structure in which Strang had his office. Several score of people had already assembled about the prison and stood chatting with that tense interest and anticipation with which the mob always awaits public infliction of the law's penalties. A third of them were women. As Nathaniel had previously noted, the feminine part of the Mormon population wore their hair either in braids down their backs or in thick curls flowing over their shoulders and with the exception of three or four were attired in skirts that just concealed their knees. Obadiah halted his companion close to a group of half a dozen of these women and nudged him slyly.

" Pretty sight, eh, Nat? " he chuckled. " Ah, the king has a wonderful eye for beauty, Nat — wonderful eye! He orders that no skirt shall fall below the female knee. Ho, ho, if he dared, if he *quite* dared, Nat! "

He nudged Nathaniel again with such enthusiasm that the latter jumped as though a knife had been thrust between his ribs.

" By George, I admire his taste! " he laughed. The women caught him staring at them, and one, who was the youngest and prettiest of the lot, smiled invitingly.

THE WHIPPING

" Tush — the Jezebel! " snapped Obadiah, catching the look. " That's her child playing just beyond."

The young woman tossed her head and her white teeth gleamed in a laugh, as though she had overheard the old councilor's words.

" See her twist her hair," he snarled venomously as the young woman, still boldly eying Nathaniel, played with the luxuriant curls that glistened in the sun upon her breast. " Ezra Wilton is so fond of her that he will take no other wife. Ugh, Strang is a fool! "

Nathaniel turned away from the smiling eyes with a shrug.

" Why? "

" To tell our women that it helps to save their souls to wear short skirts and let their hair hang down. For every soul of a woman that it saves it sends two men on the road to hell! "

So intense was the old man's displeasure and so ludicrous the twisting contortions of his face that Nathaniel could hardly restrain himself from bursting into a roar of laughter. Obadiah perceived his inclination and with an angry bob of his head led the way through to the inner edge of the waiting circle of men. Within this circle, in a small open space, was a short post with straps attached to an arm nailed across it, and leaning upon this post in an attitude of one who possesses a most distinguished office was a young man with a three thonged whip in his hand. An ominous silence pervaded the circle, with the exception of the hushed whispering of a number of women who had forced themselves into the line of spectators, bent upon witnessing the sight of blood as well as hearing the sound of lashes. Nathaniel noticed that most of the women hung in frightened curiosity beyond the men.

"That is MacDougall with the lash — official whipper and caretaker of the slave hounds," explained Obadiah in a whisper.

Nathaniel gave a start of horror.

"Slave hounds!" he breathed.

The councilor grinned and twisted his hands in enjoyment of his companion's surprise.

" We have the finest pack of bloodhounds north of Louisiana," he continued, so low that only Nathaniel could hear. " See! Isn't the earth worn smooth and hard about that post? "

Nathaniel looked and his blood grew hot.

" I have seen such things in the South," he said. " But not — for white men! "

The councilor caught him by the arm.

" They are coming! "

In the direction of the jail the crowd was separating. Men crushed back on each side, forming a narrow aisle, even the whispering of the women ceased. A moment later three men appeared in the opening between the spectators. One of these, who walked between the other two, was stripped to the waist. About each of his naked wrists was tied a leather thong and these thongs were held by the man's guards. The prisoner's face was livid; his hands were red with blood that dripped from his lacerated wrists;

his eyes glared malignantly and his heaving chest showed that he had not been brought from the log prison without a struggle.

"Ah, it's Wittle first!" breathed the councilor. "It's he who said his wife should not wear short skirts."

At the edge of the circle the prisoner hesitated and the muscles in his arms and chest grew rigid. Those of the crowd nearest to him drew back. Then a sudden change swept over the man's features and he walked quickly to the stake and kneeled before it. The thongs about his wrists were tied to the straps of the cross-piece and the whipper took his position. As the first lash fell, a cry burst from the lips of the victim. When the whip descended again he was silent. A curious sensation of sickness crept over Nathaniel as he saw the red gashes thicken on the white flesh. Five times — six times — seven times the whip rose and fell and he could see the blood starting. In horror he turned his eyes away. Behind him a man grinned at the whiteness of his face and the involuntary trembling of his lips. Again and again he heard the lash fall upon the naked back. From near him there came the sobbing moan of a woman. A subdued movement, a sound as of murmuring wordless voices swept through the throng. A steady glitter filled the eyes of the man who had laughed at him — and he turned again to the stake. The man's back was dripping blood. Great red seams lay upon his shoulders and a single lash had cut his bowed neck. Another stroke, more fierce than the others, and MacDougall turned away from the figure at the post, breathing hard. The guards unfastened the victim's wrist-thongs and the man staggered to his feet. As he swayed down through the path that opened for him his crimson back shone in the sun.

" Great God! " gasped Nathaniel.

He turned to Obadiah and was startled by the appearance of the old man. The councilor's face was ghastly. His mouth twitched and his body trembled. Nathaniel took his arm sympathetically.

"Hadn't we better go, Dad?" he whispered.

"No — no — no — not yet, Nat. It's — it's — Neil now and I must see how the boy — stands it!"

It was but a short time before the guards returned. This time their prisoner walked free and erect. The thongs dangled from his wrists and he was a pace ahead of the two men who accompanied him. He was a young man. Nathaniel judged his age at twenty-five. He was a striking contrast to the man who had suffered first at the post. His face instead of betraying the former's pallor was flushed with excitement; his head was held high; not a sign of fear or hesitation shone in his eyes. As he glanced quickly around the circle of faces the flush grew deeper in his cheeks. He nodded and smiled at MacDougall and in that nod and smile there was a meaning that sent a shiver to the whipmaster's heart. Then his eyes fell upon Obadiah and Nathaniel. He saw the councilor's hand resting upon the young captain's arm and a flash of understanding passed over his face. For an instant the eyes of the two young men met. The man at the post took half a step forward. His lips moved as if he was on the point of speaking, the defiant smile went out of his face, the flush faded in his cheeks. Then he turned quickly and held out his hands to the guards.

As the young man kneeled before the post Nathaniel heard a smothered sob at his side which he knew came from Obadiah.

"Come, Dad," he said softly. "I can't stand this. Let's get away!"

He shoved the councilor back. The lash whistled through the air behind him. As it fell there came a piercing cry. It was a woman's voice, and with a snarl like that of a tortured animal the old man struck down Nathaniel's arm and clawed his way back to the edge of the line. On the opposite side there was a surging in the crowd and as MacDougall raised his whip a woman burst through.

"My God!" cried Nathaniel, "it's —"

He left the rest of the words unspoken. His veins leaped with fire. A single sweep of his powerful arms and he had forced himself through the innermost line of spectators. Within a dozen feet of him stood Strang's wife, her beautiful hair disheveled, her face deadly white, her bosom heaving as if she had been running. In a moment her eyes had taken in the situation — the man at the stake, the upraised lash — and Nathaniel. With a sobbing, breathless cry, she flung herself in front of Mac-Dougall and threw her arms around the kneeling man, her hair covering him in a glistening veil. For an instant her eyes were raised to Nathaniel and he saw in them that same agonized appeal that had called to him through the king's window. The striking muscles of his arms tightened like steel. One of the guards sprang forward and caught the girl roughly by the arm

She flung herself in front of MacDougall.—*Page* 110

and attempted to drag her away. In his excitement he pulled her head back and her hair trailed in the dirt. The sight was maddening. From Nathaniel's throat there came a fierce cry and in a single leap he had cleared the distance to the guard and had driven his fist against the officer's head with the sickening force of a sledge-hammer. The man fell without a groan. In another flash he had drawn his knife and severed the thongs that held the man at the stake. For a moment his face was very near the girl's and he saw her lips form the glad cry which he did not wait to hear.

He turned like an enraged beast toward the circle of dumfounded spectators and launched himself at the second guard. From behind him there sounded a shout and he caught the gleam of naked shoulders as the man who had been at the stake rushed to his side. Together they tore through the narrow rim of the crowd, striking at the faces which appeared before them, their terrific blows driving men right and left.

"This way, Neil!" shouted Nathaniel. "This way — to the ship!"

They raced up the slope that led from the town to the forest. Even the king's officer, palsied by the suddenness of the attack, had not followed. From a screened window in the king's building two men had witnessed the exciting scene near the jail. One of these men was Strang. The other was Arbor Croche. At another window a few feet away, hidden from their eyes by a high desk and masses of papers and books, Winnsome Croche was crumpled up on the floor hardly daring to breathe through fear of betraying her presence. From these windows they had seen the girl run from behind the jail; they had watched her struggle through the line of spectators, saw Nathaniel leap forward — saw the quick blow, the gleaming knife, and the escape. So suddenly had it all occurred that not a sound escaped the two astonished men. But as Nathaniel and Neil burst through the crowd and sped toward the forest Strang's great voice boomed forth like the rumble of a gun.

"Arbor Croche, overtake those men — and kill them!"

With a wild curse the chief of sheriffs dashed down the stairway and as she heard him go the terror of Winnsome's heart seemed to turn her blood cold. She knew what that command meant. She knew that her father would obey it. As the daughter of the chief of sheriffs more than one burning secret was hidden in her breast, more than one of those frightful daggers that had pricked at the soul of her mother until they had murdered her. And the chief of them all was this: that to Arbor Croche the words of Strang were the words of God and that if the prophet said kill, he would kill. For a full minute she crouched in her concealment, stunned by the horror that had so quickly taken the place of the joy with which she had witnessed the escape. She heard Strang leave the window, heard his heavy steps in the outer room, heard the door close, and knew that he, too, was gone.

She sprang to her feet and ran to the window at which the two men had stood. The chief of sheriffs was already at the jail. The crowd had begun to disperse. Men were swarming like ants up the long slope reaching to the forest. Three or four of the leaders were running and she knew that they were hot in pursuit of the fugitives. Others were following more slowly and among these she saw that there were women. As she looked there came a sound from the stair. She recognized the step. She recognized the voice that called her name a moment later and with a despairing cry she turned with outstretched arms to greet the girl for whom Nathaniel had interrupted the king's whipping.

CHAPTER V

HARDLY had Nathaniel fought his way through the thin crowd of startled spectators about the whipping-post before the enormity of his offense in interrupting the king's justice dawned upon him. He was not sorry that he had responded to the mute appeal of the girl who had entered so strangely into his life. He rejoiced at the spirit that had moved him to action, that had fired his blood and put the strength of a giant in his arms; and his nerves tingled with an unreasoning joy that he had leaped all barriers which in cooler moments would have restrained him, and which fixed in his excited brain only the memory of the beautiful face that had sought his own in those crucial moments of its suffering. The girl had turned to him and to him alone among all those men. He had heard her voice, he had felt the soft sweep of her hair as he severed the prisoner's thongs, he had caught the flash of her eyes and the movement of her lips as he dashed himself into the crowd. And as he sped swiftly up the slope he considered himself amply repaid for all that he had done. His blood was stirred as if by the fire of sharp wines; he was still in a tension of fighting excitement. Yet no sooner had he fought himself clear of the mob than his better judgment leaped into the ascendency. If danger had been lurking for him before it was doubly threatening now and he was sufficiently possessed of the common spirit of self-preservation to exult at the speed with which he was enabled to leave pursuit behind. A single glance over his shoulder assured him that the man whom he had saved from the prophet's wrath was close at his heels. His first impulse was to direct his flight toward Obadiah's cabin; his second to follow the path that led to his ship.

At this hour some of his men would surely be awaiting him in a small boat and once aboard the *Typhoon* he could continue his campaign against the Mormon king with better chances of success than as a lone fugitive on the island. Besides, he knew what Casey would do at sundown.

At the top of the slope he stopped and waited for the other to come up to him.

" I've got a ship off there," he called, pointing inland. " Take a short cut for the point at the head of the island. There's a boat waiting for us! "

Neil came up panting. He was breathing so hard that for a moment he found it impossible to speak but in his eyes there was a look that told his unbounded gratitude. They were clear, fearless eyes, with the blue glint of steel in them and, as he held out his hands to Nathaniel, they were luminous with the joy of his deliverance.

" Thank you, Captain Plum! "

He spoke his companion's name with the assurance of one who had known it for a long time. "If they loose the dogs there will be no time for the ship," he added, with a suggestive hunch of his naked shoulders. "Follow me!"

There was no alarm in his voice and Nathaniel caught the flashing gleam of white teeth as Neil smiled grimly back at him, running in the lead. From the man's eyes the master of the *Typhoon* had sized up his companion as a fighter. The smile — daring, confident, and yet signaling their danger — assured him that he was right, and he followed close behind without question. A dozen rods up the path Neil turned into a dense thicket of briars and underbrush and for ten minutes they plunged through the pathless jungle. Now and then Nathaniel saw the three red stripes of the whipper's lash upon the bare shoulders of the man ahead and to these every step seemed to add new wounds made by the thorns. As they came out upon an old roadway the captain stripped off his coat and Neil thrust himself into it as they ran.

Even in these first minutes of their flight Nathaniel was thrilled by another thought than that of the peril behind them. Whom had he saved? Who was this clear-eyed young fellow for whom the girl had so openly sacrificed herself at the whipping-post, about whom she had thrown her arms and covered with the protection of her glorious hair? With his joy at having served her there was mingled a chilling doubt as these questions formed themselves in his mind. Obadiah's vague suggestions, the scene in the king's room, the night visits of the girl to the councilor's cabin — and last of all this incident at the jail flashed upon him now with another meaning, with a significance that slowly cooled the enthusiasm in his veins. He was sure that he was near the solution of the mysterious events in which he had become involved, and yet this knowledge brought with it something of apprehension, something which made him anticipate and yet dread the moment when the fugitive ahead would stop in his flight, and he might ask him those questions which would at least relieve him of his burden of doubt. They had traveled a mile through forest unbroken by path or road when Neil halted on the edge of a little stream that ran into a swamp. Pointing into the tangled fen with a confident smile he plunged to his waist in the water and waded slowly through the slough into the gloom of the densest alder. A few minutes later he turned in to the shore and the soft bog gave place to firm ground. Before Nathaniel had cleared the stream he saw his companion drop to his knees beside a fallen log and when he came up to him he was unwrapping a piece of canvas from about a gun. With a warning gesture he rose to his feet and for twenty seconds the men stood and listened. No sound came to them but the chirp of a startled squirrel and the barking of a dog in the direction of St. James.

" They haven't turned out the dogs yet," said Neil, holding a hand against his heaving chest. " If they do they can't reach us through that slough." He leaned his rifle against the log and again thrusting an arm into the place where it had been concealed drew forth a small box.

"Powder and ball — and grub!" he laughed. "You see I am a sort of revolutionist and have my hiding-places. To-morrow — I will be a martyr." He spoke as quietly as though his words but carried a careless jest.

"A martyr?" laughed Nathaniel, looking down into the smiling, sweating face.

"Yes, to-morrow I shall kill Strang."

There was no excitement in Neil's voice as he stood erect. The smile did not leave his lips. But in his eyes there shone that which neither words nor smiling lips revealed, a reckless, blazing fury hidden deep in them — so deep that Nathaniel stared to assure himself what it was. The other saw the doubt in his face.

"To-morrow I shall kill Strang," he repeated. "I shall kill him with this gun from under the window of his house through which you saw Marion."

"Marion!" exclaimed Nathaniel. "Marion—" He leaned forward eagerly, questioning. "Tell me —"

"My sister, Captain Plum!"

It seemed to Nathaniel that every fiber in his body was stretched to the breaking point. He reached out, dazed by what he had heard and with both hands seized Neil's arm.

"Your sister — who came to you at the whipping-post?"

"That was Marion."

"And — Strang's wife?"

"No!" cried Neil. "No — not his wife!" He drew back from Nathaniel's touch as if the question had stabbed him to the heart. The passion that had slumbered in his eyes burst into savage flame and his face became suddenly terrible to look upon. There was hatred there such as Nathaniel had never seen; a ferocious, pitiless hatred that sent a shuddering thrill through him as he stood before it. After a moment the clenched fist that had risen above Neil's head dropped to his side. Half apologetically he held out his hand to his companion.

" Captain Plum, we've got a lot to thank you for, Marion and I," he said, a tremble of the passing emotion in his voice. " Obadiah told Marion that help might come to us through you and Marion brought the word to me at the jail late last night — after she had seen you at the window. The old councilor kept his word! You have saved her ! "

" Saved her ! " gasped Nathaniel. " From what? How? " A hundred questions seemed leaping from his heart to his lips.

" From Strang. Good God, don't you understand? I tell you that I am going to kill Strang ! "

Neil stood as though appalled by his companion's incomprehension. " I am going to kill Strang, I tell you ! " he cried again, the fire burning deeper through the sweat of his cheeks.

Nathaniel's bewilderment still shone in his face.

" She is not Strang's wife," he spoke softly, as if to himself. " And she is not —" His face flushed as he nearly spoke the words. " Obadiah lied!" He looked squarely into Neil's eyes. " No, I don't understand you. The councilor said that she — that Marion was Strang's wife. He told me nothing more than that, nothing of her trouble, nothing about you. Until this moment I have been completely mystified. Only her eyes led me to do — what I did at the jail."

Neil gazed at him in astonishment.

" Obadiah told — you — nothing? " he asked incredulously.

" Not a word about you or Marion except that Marion was the king's seventh wife. But he hinted at many things and kept me on the trail, always expecting, always watching, and yet every hour was one of mystery. I am in the darkest of it at this instant. What does it all mean? Why are you going to kill Strang? Why —"

Neil interrupted him with a cry so poignant

124

in its wretchedness that the last question died upon his lips.

"I thought that the councilor had told you all," he said. "I thought you knew." The disappointment in his voice was almost despair. "Then — it was only accidentally — you helped us?"

"Only accidentally that I helped *you* — yes! But Marion —" Nathaniel crushed Neil's hand in both his own and his eyes betrayed more than he would have said. "I've got an armed ship and a dozen men out there and if I can help Marion by blowing up St. James — I'll do it!"

For a time only the tense breathing of the two broke the silence of their lips. They looked into each other's face, Nathaniel with all the eagerness of the passion with which Marion had stirred his soul, Neil half doubting, as if he were trying to find in this man's eyes the friendship which he had not questioned a few minutes before.

" Obadiah told you nothing? " he asked again, as if still unbelieving.

" Nothing."

" And you have not seen Marion — to talk with her? "

" No."

Nathaniel had dropped his companion's hand, and now Neil walked to the log and sat down with his face turned in the direction from which their pursuers must come if they entered the swamp.

Suddenly the memory of Obadiah's note shot into Nathaniel's head, the councilor's admonition, his allusion to a visitor. With this memory there recurred to him Obadiah's words at the temple, " If you had remained at the cabin, Nat, you would have known that I was your friend. She would have come to you, but now — it is impossible." For the first time the truth' began to dawn upon him. He went and sat down beside Neil.

" I am beginning to understand — a little,"

he said. " Obadiah had planned that I should meet Marion, but I was a fool and spoiled his scheme. If I had done as he told me I should have seen her this morning."

In a few words he reviewed the events of the preceding evening and of that morning — of his coming to the island, his meeting with Obadiah, and of the singular way in which he had become interested in Marion. He omitted the oaths but told of Winnsome's warning and of his interview with the Mormon king. When he spoke of the girl as he had seen her through the king's window, and of her appealing face turned to him at the jail, his voice trembled with an excitement that deepened the flush in Neil's cheeks.

" Captain Plum, I thank God that you like Marion," he said simply. " After I kill Strang will you help her? "

" Yes."

" You are willing to risk —"

" My life — my men — my ship! "

Nathaniel spoke like one to whom there had

been suddenly opened the portals to a great joy. He sprang to his feet and stood before Neil, his whole being throbbing with the emotions which had been awakened within him.

"Good God, why don't you tell me what her peril is?" he cried, no longer restraining himself. "Why are you going to kill Strang? Has he — has he —" His face flamed with the question which he dared not finish.

"No — not that!" interrupted Neil. "He has never laid a hand on Marion. She hates him as she hates the snakes in this swamp. And yet — next Sunday she is to become his seventh wife!"

Nathaniel started as if he had been threatened by a blow.

"You mean — he is forcing her into his harem?" he asked.

"No, he can not do that!" exclaimed Neil, the hatred bursting out anew in his face. "He can not force her into marrying him, and yet —" He flung his arms above his head in sudden passionate despair. " As there is a God in Heaven I would give ten years of my life for the secret of the prophet's power over Marion!" he groaned. " Three months ago her hatred of him was terrible. She loathed the sight of him. I have seen her shiver at the sound of his voice. When he asked her to become his wife she refused him in words that I had believed no person in the kingdom would dared to have used. Then — less than a month ago — the change came, and one day she told me that she had made up her mind to become Strang's wife. From that day her heart was broken. I was dumfounded. I raged and cursed and even threatened. Once I accused her of a shameful thing and though I implored her forgiveness a thousand times I know that she weeps over my brutal words still. But nothing could change her. On my knees I have pleaded with her, and once she flung her arms round my shoulders and said, ' Neil, I can not tell you why I am marrying Strang. But I must.' I went to Strang and demanded an explanation; I told him that my sister hated him, that the sight of his face and the sound of his voice filled her with abhorrence, but he only laughed at me and asked why I objected to becoming the brother-in-law of a prophet. Day by day I have seen Marion's soul dying within her. Some terrible secret is gnawing at her heart, robbing her of the very life which a few weeks ago made her the most beautiful thing on this island; some dreadful influence is shadowing her every step, and as the day draws near when she is to join the king's harem I see in her eyes at times a look that frightens me. There is only one salvation. To-morrow I shall kill Strang!"

" And then? "

Neil shrugged his shoulders.

" I will shoot him through the abdomen so that he will live to tell his wives who did the deed. After that I will try to make my escape to the mainland."

" And Marion —"

" Will not marry Strang! Isn't that plain? "

" You have guessed nothing — no cause for the prophet's power over your sister? " asked Nathaniel.

" Absolutely nothing. And yet that influence is such that at times the thought of it freezes the blood in my veins. It is so great that Strang did not hesitate to throw me into jail on the pretext that I had threatened his life. Marion implored him to spare me the disgrace of a public whipping and he replied by reading to her the commandments of the kingdom. That was last night — when you saw her through the window. Strang is madly infatuated with her beauty and yet he dares to go to any length without fear of losing her. She has become his slave. She is as completely in his power as though bound in iron chains. And the most terrible thing about it all is that she has constantly urged me to leave the island — to go, and never return. Great God, what does it all mean? I love her more than anything else on earth, we have been inseparable since the day she was old enough to toddle alone — and yet she would have me leave her! No power on earth can reveal the secret that is torturing her. No power can make Strang divulge it."

"And Obadiah Price!" cried Nathaniel, sudden excitement flashing in his eyes. "Does he not know?"

"I believe that he does!" replied Neil, pacing back and forth in his agitation. "Captain Plum, if there is a man on this island who loves Marion with all of a father's devotion it is Obadiah Price, and yet he swears that he knows nothing of the terrible influence which has so suddenly enslaved her to the prophet! He suggests that it may be mesmerism, but I —". He interrupted himself with a harsh, mirthless laugh. "Mesmerism be damned! It's not that!"

"Your sister — is — a Mormon," ventured Nathaniel, remembering what the prophet had said to him that morning. "Could it be her faith?— a message revealed through Strang from —"

Neil stopped him almost fiercely.

" Marion is not a Mormon ! " he said.   " She hates Mormonism as she hates Strang.   I have tried to get her to leave the island with me but she insists on staying because of the old folk. They are very old, Captain Plum, and they believe in the prophet and his Heaven as you and I believe in that blue sky up there.   The day before I was arrested I begged my sister to flee to the mainland with me but she refused with the words that she had said to me a hundred times before — ' Neil, I must marry the prophet ! '   Don't you see there is nothing to do — but to kill Strang ? "

Nathaniel thrust his hand into a pocket of the coat he had loaned to Neil and drew forth his pipe and tobacco pouch.   As he loaded the pipe he looked squarely into the other's eyes and smiled.

" Neil," he said softly.   " Do you know that

you would have made an awful fool of yourself if I hadn't hove in sight just when I did? "

He lighted his pipe with exasperating coolness, still smiling over its bowl.

" You are not going to kill Strang to-morrow," he added, throwing away the match and placing both hands on Neil's shoulders. His eyes were laughing with the joy that shone in them. " Neil, I am ashamed of you! You have worried a devilish lot over a very simple matter. See here —" He blew a cloud of smoke over the other's head. " I've learned to demand some sort of pay for my services since I landed on this island. Will you promise to be — a sort of brother — to me — if I steal Marion and sail away with her to-night? "

CHAPTER VI

MARION

At Nathaniel's astonishing words Neil stood as though struck suddenly dumb.

" Don't you see what a very simple case it is? " he continued, enjoying the other's surprised silence. " You plan to kill Strang to keep Marion from marrying him. Well, I will hunt up Marion, put her in a bag if necessary, and carry her to my ship. Isn't that better and safer and just as sure as murder? "

The excitement had gone out of Neil's face. The flush slowly faded from his cheeks and in his eyes there gleamed something besides the malevolence of a few moments before. As Nathaniel stepped back from him half laughing and puffing clouds of smoke from his pipe Marion's brother thrust his hands into his pockets with an exclamation that forcefully expressed his appreciation of Captain Plum's scheme.

" I never thought of that," he added, after a moment. " By Heaven, it will be easy —"

" So easy that I tell you again I am ashamed of you for not having thought of it! " cried Nathaniel. " The first thing is to get safely aboard my ship."

" We can do that within an hour."

" And to-night — where will we find Marion? "

" At home," said Neil. " We live near Obadiah. You must have seen the house as you came out into the clearing this morning from the forest."

Nathaniel smiled as he thought of his suspicions of the old councilor.

" It couldn't be better situated for our work," he said. " Does the forest run down to the lake on Obadiah's side of the island? "

" Clear to the beach."

Neil's face betrayed a sudden flash of doubt.

" I believe that our place has been watched for some time," he explained. " I am sure that it is especially guarded at night and that no person leaves or enters it without the knowledge of Strang. I am certain that Marion is aware of this surveillance although she professes to be wholly ignorant of it. It may cause us trouble."

" Can you reach the house without being observed? "

" After midnight — yes."

" Then there is no cause for alarm," declared Nathaniel. " If necessary I can bring ten men into the edge of the woods. Two can approach the house as quietly as one and I will go with you. Once there you can tell Marion that your life depends on her accompanying you to Obadiah's. I believe she will go. If she won't —" He stretched out his arms as if in anticipation of the burden they might hold. " If she won't — I'll help you carry her! "

" And meanwhile," said Neil, " Arbor Croche's men—"

" Will be as dead as herring floaters if they show up! " he cried, leaping two feet off the ground in his enthusiasm. " I've got twelve of the damnedest fighters aboard my ship that ever lived and ten of them will be in the edge of the woods ! "

Neil's eyes were shining with something that made Nathaniel turn his own to the loading of his pipe.

" Captain Plum, I hope I will be able to repay you for this," he said. There was a trembling break in his voice and for a moment Nathaniel did not look up. His own heart was near bursting with the new life that throbbed within it. When he raised his eyes to his companion's face again there was a light in them that spoke almost as plainly as words.

" You haven't accepted my price, yet, Neil," he replied quietly. " I asked you if you'd — be — a sort of brother —"

Neil sprang to his side with a fervor that knocked the pipe out of his hand.

" I swear that! And if Marion doesn't —"

Suddenly he jerked himself into a listening attitude.

" Hark ! "

For a moment the two ceased to breathe. The sound had come to them both, low, distant. After it there fell a brief hush. Then again, as they stared questioningly into each other's eyes, it rolled faintly into the swamp — the deep, far baying of a hound.

" Ah ! " exclaimed Neil, drawing back with a deep breath. " I thought they would do it ! "

" The bloodhounds ! "

Horror, not fear, sent an involuntary shiver through Nathaniel.

" They can't reach us ! " assured Neil. There was the glitter of triumph in his eyes. " This was to have been my way of escape after I killed Strang. A quarter of a mile deeper in the swamp I have a canoe." He picked up the

139

gun and box and began forcing his way through the dense alder along the edge of the stream. " I'd like to stay and murder those dogs," he called back, " but it wouldn't be policy."

For a time the crashing of their bodies through the dense growth of the swamp drowned all other sound. Five minutes later Neil stopped on the edge of a wide bog. The hounds were giving fierce tongue in the forest on their left and their nearness sent Nathaniel's hand to his pistol. Neil saw the movement and laughed.

" Don't like the sound, eh? " he said. " We get used to it on Beaver Island. They're just about at the place where they tore little Jim Schredder to pieces a few weeks back. Schredder tried to kill one of the elders for stealing his wife while he was away on a night's fishing trip."

He plunged to his knees in the bog.

" They caught him just before he reached the swamp," he flung back over his shoulder. " Two minutes more and he would have been safe."

Nathaniel, sinking to his knees in the mire, forged up beside him.

" Lord! " he exclaimed, as a breath of air brought a sudden burst of blood-curdling cries to them. " If they'd loosed them on us sooner —"

He shivered at the terrible grimace Neil turned on him.

" Had they slipped the leashes when we escaped, we would have been with poor Schredder now, Captain Plum. By the way — " he stopped a moment to wipe the water and mud from his face, "— three days after they covered Schredder's bones with muck out there, the elder took Schredder's wife! She was too pretty for a fisherman." He started on, but halted suddenly with uplifted hand. No longer could they hear the baying of the dogs. " They've struck the creek! " said Neil. " Listen! "

After an interval of silence there came a long mournful howl.

" Treed — treed or in the water, that's what

the howling means. How Croche and his devils
are hustling now!"

A curse was mingled with Neil's breath as he
forced his way through the bog. Twenty rods
farther on they came to a slime covered bit of
water on which was floating a dugout canoe.
Immense relief replaced the anxiety in Nathaniel's face as he climbed into it. At that moment
he was willing to fight a hundred men for
Marion's sake, but snakes and bogs and bloodhounds were entirely outside his pale of argument and he exhibited no hesitation in betraying this fact to his companion. For a quarter
of a mile Neil forced the dugout through water
viscid with slime and rotted substance before
the clearer channel of the creek was reached.
As they progressed the stream constantly became deeper and more navigable until it finally
began to show signs of a current and a little
later, under the powerful impetus of Neil's paddle, the canoe shot from between the dense shores
into the open lake. A mile away Nathaniel dis-

Neil forced the dugout through the water.—*Page* 142

cerned the point of forest beyond which the *Typhoon* was hidden. He pointed out the location of the ship to his companion.

"You are sure there is a small boat waiting for you on the point?" asked Neil.

"Yes, since early morning."

Neil was absorbed in thought for some time as he drove the canoe through the tall rice grass that grew thick along the edge of the shore.

"How would it be if I landed you on the point and met you to-night at Obadiah's?" he asked suddenly. "It is probable that after we get Marion aboard your ship I will not return to the island again, and it is quite necessary that I run down the coast for a couple of miles — for —" He did not finish his reason, but added: "I can make the whole distance in this rice so there is no danger of being seen. Or you might lie off the point yonder and I would join you early this evening."

"That would be a better plan if we must separate," said Nathaniel, whose voice betrayed the reluctance with which he assented to the project. He had guessed shrewdly at Neil's motive. " Is it possible that we may have another young lady passenger? " he asked banteringly.

There was no answering humor to this in Neil's eyes.

" I wish we might! " he said quietly.

" We can! " exclaimed Nathaniel. " My ship —"

" It is impossible. I am speaking of Winnsome. Arbor Croche's house is in the heart of the town and guarded by dogs. I doubt if she would go, anyway. She has always been like a little sister to Marion and me and she has come to believe — something — as we do. I hate to leave her."

" Obadiah told me about her mother," ventured Nathaniel. " He said that some day Winnsome will be a queen."

" I knew her mother," replied Neil, as though he had not heard Nathaniel's last words. He

looked frankly into the other's face. " I wor-
shipped her!"

" Oh-h-h! "

" From a distance," he hastened. " She was
as pure as Winnsome is now. Little Winn
looks like her. Some day she will be as beautiful."

" She is beautiful now."

" But she is a mere child. Why, it seems
only a year ago that I was toting her about on
my shoulders! And by George, that was a
year before her mother died! She is sixteen
now."

Nathaniel laughed softly.

" To-morrow she will be making love, Neil,
and before you know it she will be married and
have a family of her own. I tell you she is a
woman — and if you are not a fool you will
take her away with Marion."

With a powerful stroke of his paddle Neil
brought the canoe in to the shore.

" There! " he whispered. " You have only

to cross this point to reach your boat." He stretched out his long arm and in the silence the two shook hands. "If you should happen to think of a way — that we might get Winnsome —" he added, coloring.

The sudden grip of his companion's fingers made him flinch.

"We must!" said Nathaniel.

He climbed ashore and watched Neil until he had disappeared in the wild rice. Then he turned into the woods. He looked at his watch and saw that it was only two o'clock. He was conscious of no fatigue; he was not conscious of hunger. To him the whole world had suddenly opened with glorious promise and in the still depths of the forest he felt like singing out his rejoicing. He had never stopped to ask himself what might be the end of this passion that had overwhelmed him; he lived only in the present, in the knowledge that Marion was not a wife, and that it was he whom fate had chosen for her deliverance. He reasoned

nothing beyond the sweet eyes that had called
upon him, that had burned their gratitude, their
hope and their despair upon his soul; nothing
beyond the thought that she would soon be free
from the mysterious influence of the Mormon
king and that for days and nights after that
she would be on the same ship with him. He
had emptied the pockets of the coat he had given
Neil and now he brought forth the old letter
which Obadiah had rescued from the sands. He
read it over again as he sat for a few moments
in the cool of the forest and there was no trouble
in his face now. It was from a girl. He had
known that girl, years ago, as Neil knew Winnsome; in years of wandering he had almost forgotten her — until this letter came. It had
brought many memories back to him with shock-
ing clearness. The old folk were still in the
little home under the hill; they received his let-
ters; they received the money he sent them each
month — but they wanted *him*. The girl wrote
with merciless candor. He had been away four

years and it was time for him to return. She told him why. She wrote what they, in their loving fear of inflicting pain, would never have dared to say. At the end, in a postscript, she had asked for his congratulations on her approaching marriage.

To Nathaniel this letter had been a torment. He saw the truth as he had never seen it before — that his place was back there in Vermont, with his father and mother; and that there was something unpleasant in thinking of the girl as belonging to another. But now matters had changed. The letter was a hope and inspiration to him and he smoothed it out with tender care. What a refuge that little home among the Vermont hills would make for Marion! He trembled at the thought and his heart sang with the promise of it as he went his way again through the thick growth of the woods.

It was half an hour before he came out upon the beach. Eagerly he scanned the sea. The

Typhoon was nowhere in sight and for an in
stant the gladness that had been in his heart
gave place to a chilling fear. But the direction of the wind reassured him. Casey had probably moved beyond the jutting promontory, that
swung in the form of a cart wheel from the base
of the point, that he might have sea room in
case of something worse than a stiff breeze.
But where was the small boat? With every
step adding to his anxiety Nathaniel hurried
along the narrow rim of beach. He went to
the very tip of the point which reached out like
the white forefinger of a lady's hand into the
sea; he passed the spot where he had lain concealed the preceding day; his breath came faster
and faster; he ran, and called softly, and at last
halted in the arch of the cart wheel with the
fear full-flaming in his breast. Over all those
miles of sea there was no sign of the sloop.
From end to end of the point there was no boat.
What did it mean? Breathlessly he tore his way
through the strip of forest on the promontory

until all Lake Michigan to the south lay before his eyes. The *Typhoon* was gone! Was it possible that Casey had abandoned hope of Nathaniel's return and was already lying off St. James with shotted gun? The thought sent a shiver of despair through him. He passed to the opposite side of the point and followed it foot by foot, but there was no sign of life, no distant flash of white that might have been the canvas of the sloop *Typhoon.*

There was only one thing for him to do — wait. So he went to his hiding-place of the day before and watched the sea with staring eyes. An hour passed and his still aching vision saw no sign of sail; two hours — and the sun was falling in a blinding glare over the Wisconsin wilderness. At last he sprang to his feet with a hopeless cry and stood for a few moments undecided. Should he wait until night with the hope of attracting the attention of Neil and joining him in his canoe or should he hasten in the direction of St. James? In the darkness he might miss Neil, unless he kept up a constant shouting, which would probably bring the Mormons down upon him; if he went to St. James there was a possibility of reaching Casey. He still had faith in Obadiah and he was sure that the old man would help him to reach his ship; he might even assist him in his scheme of getting Marion from the island.

He would go to the councilor's. Having once decided, Nathaniel turned in the direction of the town, avoiding the use of the path which he and Obadiah had taken, but following in the forest near enough to use it as a guide. He was confident that Arbor Croche and his sheriffs were confining their man-hunt to the swamp, but in spite of this belief he exercised extreme caution, stopping to listen now and then, with one hand always near his pistol. A quiet gloom filled the forest and by the tree-tops he marked the going down of the sun. Nathaniel's ears ached with their strain of listening for the rumbling roar that would tell of Casey's attack on St. James.

Suddenly he heard a crackling in the under-brush ahead of him, a sound that came not from the strain of listening for the rumbling roar and in a moment he had dodged into the con-cealment of the huge roots of an overturned tree, drawn pistol in hand. Whatever object was approaching came slowly, as if hesitating at each step — a cautious, stealthy advance, it struck Nathaniel, and he cocked his weapon. Directly in front of him, half a stone's throw away, was a dense growth of hazel and he could see the tops of the slender bushes swaying. Twice this movement ceased and the second time there came a crashing of brush and a faint cry. For many minutes after that there was abso-lute silence. Was it the cry of an animal that he had heard — or of a man? In either case the creature who made it had fallen in the thicket and was lying there as still as if dead. For a quarter of an hour Nathaniel waited and lis-tened. He could no longer have seen the move-ment of bushes in the gathering night-gloom of the forest but his ears were strained to catch the slightest sound from the direction of the mysterious thing that lay within less than a dozen rods of him. Slowly he drew himself out from the shelter of the roots and advanced step by step. Half way to the thicket a stick cracked loudly under his foot and as the sound startled the dead quiet of the forest with pistol-shot clearness there came another cry from the dense hazel, a cry which was neither that of man nor animal but of a woman; and with an answering shout Nathaniel sprang forward to meet there in the edge of the thicket the white face and outstretched arms of Marion. The girl was swaying on her feet. In her face there was a pallor that even in his instant's glance sent a chill of horror through the man and as she staggered toward him, half falling, her lips weakly forming his name Nathaniel leaped to her and caught her close in his arms. In that moment something seemed to burst within him and flood his veins with fire. Closer he held the girl, and heavier he knew that she was becoming in his arms. Her head was upon his breast, his face was crushed in her hair, he felt her throbbing and breathing against him and his lips quivered with the words that were bursting for freedom in his soul. But first there came the girl's own whispered breath — " Neil — where is Neil? "

" He is gone — gone from the island! "

She had become a dead weight now and so he knelt on the ground with her, her head still upon his breast, her eyes closed, her arms fallen to her side. And as Nathaniel looked into the face from which all life seemed to have fled he forgot everything but the joy of this moment — forgot all in life but this woman against his breast. He kissed her soft mouth and the closed eyes until the eyes themselves opened again and gazed at him in a startled, half understanding way, until he drew his head far back with the shame of what he had dared to do flaming in his face.

And as for another moment he held her thus, feeling the quivering life returning in her, there

came to him through that vast forest stillness
the distant deep-toned thunder of a great gun.

"That's Casey!" he whispered close down to
the girl's face. His voice was almost sobbing
in its happiness. "That's Casey — firing on
St. James!"

CHAPTER VII

THE HOUR OF VENGEANCE

For perhaps twenty seconds after the last echoes of the gun had rolled through the forest the girl lay passive in Nathaniel's arms, so close that he could feel her heart beating against his own and her breath sweeping his face. Then there came a pressure against his breast, a gentle resistance of Marion's half conscious form, and when she had awakened from her partial swoon he was holding her in the crook of his arm. It had all passed quickly, the girl had rested against him only so long as he might have held half a dozen breaths and yet there had been all of a lifetime in it for Nathaniel Plum, a cycle of joy that he knew would remain with him for ever. But there was something bitter-sweet in the thought that she was conscious of what he had

156

done, something of humiliation as well as gladness, and still not enough of the first to make him regret that he had kissed her, that he had kissed her mouth and her eyes. He loved her, and he was glad that in those passing moments he had betrayed himself. For the first time he noticed that her face was scratched and that the sleeves of her thin waist were torn to shreds; and as she drew away from him, steadying herself with a hand on his arm, his lips were parched of words, and yet he leaned to her eagerly, everything that he would have said burning in the love of his eyes. Still irresolute in her faintness the girl smiled at him, and in that smile there was gentle accusation, the sweetness of forgiveness, and measureless gratitude, and it was yet light enough for him to see that with these there had come also a flush into her cheeks and a dazzling glow into her eyes.

" Neil has escaped! " she breathed. " And you —"

" I was going back to you, Marion! " He

spoke the words hardly above a whisper. The beautiful eyes so close to him drew his secret from him before he had thought. " I am going to take you from the island!"

With his words there came again that sound of a great gun rolling from the direction of St. James. With a frightened cry the girl staggered to her feet, and as she stood swaying unsteadily, her arms half reached to him, Nathaniel saw only mortal dread in the whiteness of her face.

" Why didn't you go? Why didn't you go with Neil?" she moaned. Her breath was coming in sobbing excitement. " Your ship is — at — St. James!"

" Yes, my ship is at St. James, Marion!" His voice was tremulous with triumph, with gladness, with a tenderness which he could not control. He put an arm half round her waist to support her trembling form and to his joy she did not move away from him. His hand was buried in the richness of her loose hair. He bent until his lips touched her silken tresses. "Neil has told me everything — about you," he added softly. "My ship is bombarding St. James, and I am going to take you from the island!"

Not until then did Marion free herself from his arm and then so gently that when she stood facing him he felt no reproof. No longer did shame send a flush into his face. He had spoken his love, though not in words, and he knew that the girl understood him. It did not occur to him in these moments that he had known this girl for only a few hours, that until now a word had never passed between them. He was conscious only that he had loved her from the time he saw her through the king's window, that he had risked his life for her, and that she knew why he had leaped into the arena at the whipping-post.

The words she spoke now came like a dash of cold water in his face.

"Your ship is not bombarding St. James, Captain Plum!" she exclaimed. Darkness hid the terror in her face but he could hear the tremble of it in her voice. "The *Typhoo*n has been captured by the Mormons and those guns are — guns of triumph — and not —" She caught her breath in a convulsive sob. "I want you to go — I want you to go — with Neil!" she pleaded.

"So Casey is taken!"

He spoke slowly, as if he had not heard her last words. For a moment he stood silent, and as silently the girl stood and watched him. She guessed the despair that was raging in his heart but when he spoke to her she could detect none of it in his voice.

"Casey is a fool," he said, unconsciously repeating Obadiah's words. "Marion, will you come with me? Will you leave the island — and join your brother?"

The hope that had risen in his heart was crushed as Marion drew farther away from him.

"You must go alone," she replied. With a powerful effort she steadied her voice. "Tell Neil that he has been condemned to death. Tell

160

him that — if he loves me — he will not return to the island."

" And I? "

From her distance she saw his arms stretched like shadows toward her.

" And you —"

Her voice was low, so low that he could hardly hear the words she spoke, but its sweetness thrilled him.

" And you — if you love me — will do this thing for me. Go to Neil. Save his life for me! "

She had come to him through the gloom, and in the luster of the eyes that were turned up to him Nathaniel saw again the power that swayed his soul.

" You will go? "

" I will save your brother — if I can! "

" You can — you can —" she breathed. In an ecstasy of gratitude she seized one of his hands in both her own. " You can save him! "

" For you — I will try."

" For me —"

She was so close that he could feel the throbbing of her bosom. Suddenly he lifted his free hand and brushed back the thick hair from her brow and turned her face until what dim light there still remained of the day glowed in the beauty of her eyes. " I will keep him from the island if I can," he said, looking deep into them, " and as there is a God in Heaven I swear that you —"

" What? " she urged, as he hesitated.

" That you shall not marry Strang ! " he finished.

A cry welled up in the girl's throat. Was it of gladness? Was it of hope? She sprang back a pace from Nathaniel and with clenched hands waited breathlessly, as if she expected him to say more.

" No — no — you can not save me from Strang ! Now — you must go ! "

She retreated slowly in the direction of the path. In an instant Nathaniel was at her side.

" I am going to see you safely back in St. James," he declared. " Then I will go to your brother."

She barred his way defiantly.

" You can not go! "

" Why? "

" Because —" He caught the frightened flutter of her voice again. " Because — they will kill you! "

The low laugh that he breathed in her hair was more of joy than fear.

" I am glad you care — Marion." He spoke her name with faltering tenderness, and led her out into the path.

" You must go," she still persisted.

" With you — yes," he answered.

She surrendered to the determination in his voice and they moved slowly along the path, listening for any sound that might come from ahead of them. Nathaniel had already formed his plan of action. From Marion's words and the voice in which she had uttered them he knew

that it would be useless for him as it had been
for Neil to urge her to flee from the island.
There remained but one thing for him to do, so
he fell back upon the scheme which he had pro-
posed to Marion's brother. He realized now
that he might be compelled to play the game
single-handed unless he could secure assistance
from Obadiah. His ship and men were in the
hands of the Mormons; Neil, in his search for
the captured vessel, stood a large chance of missing him that night, and in that event Marion's
fate would depend on him alone. If he could
locate a small boat on the beach back of Obadiah's; if he could in some way lure Marion to
it — He gave an involuntary shudder at the
thought of using force upon the girl at his side,
at the thought of her terror of those first few moments, her struggles, her broken confidence.
She believed in him now. She believed that he
loved her. She trusted him. The warm soft
pressure of her hand as it clung to his arm in
the blackening gloom of the forest was evidence

of that trust. She looked into his face anxiously, inquiringly when they stopped to listen, like a child who was sure of a stronger spirit at her side. She held her breath when he held his, she listened when he listened, her feet fell with velvet stillness when he stepped with caution. Her confidence in him was like a beautiful dream to Nathaniel and he trembled when he pictured the destruction of it. After a little he reached over and as if by accident touched the hand that was lying on his arm; he dared more after a moment, and drew the warm little fingers into his great strong palm and held them there, his soul thrilled by their gentle submissiveness. And then in another breath there came to still his joy a thought of the terrible power that chained this girl to the Mormon king. He longed to speak words of encouragement to her, to instil hope in her bosom, to ask her to confide in him the secret of the shadow which hung over her, but the memory of what Neil had said to him held his lips closed.

They had walked in silence for many minutes when the girl stopped.

"It is not very far now," she whispered. "You must go!"

"Only a little farther," he begged.

She surrendered again, hesitatingly, and they went on, more slowly than before, until they came to where the path met the footway that led to Obadiah's.

"Now — now you *must* go," whispered Marion again.

In this last moment Nathaniel crushed her hand against his breast, his body throbbing with a wild tumult, and a half of what he had meant not to say fell passionately from his lips.

"Forgive me for — that — back there — Marion," he whispered. "It was because I love you — love you —" He freed her hand and stood back, choking the words that would have revealed his secret. He lied now for the love of this girl. "Neil is out there waiting for me in a small boat," he continued, pointing be-

166

yond Obadiah's to the lake. "I will see him soon, and then I will return to Obadiah's to tell you if he has left for the mainland. Will you promise to meet me there — to-night?"

"I will promise."

"At midnight —"

"Yes, at twelve o'clock."

This time it was Marion who came to him. Her eyes shone like stars.

"And if you make Neil go to the mainland," she said softly, "when I meet you I will — will tell you — something."

The last word came in a breathless sob. As she slipped into the path that led to St. James she paused for a moment and called back, in a low voice, "Tell Neil that he must go for Winnsome's sake. Tell him that her fate is shortly to be as cruel as mine — tell him that Winnsome loves him, and that she will escape and come to him on the mainland. Tell him to go — go!"

She turned again, and Nathaniel stood like a statue, hardly breathing, until the sound of her feet had died away. Then he walked swiftly up the foot-path that led to Obadiah's. He forgot his own danger in the excitement that pulsated with every fiber of his being, forgot his old caution and the fears that gave birth to it — forgot everything in those moments but Marion and his own great happiness. Neil's absence meant nothing to him now. He had held Marion in his arms, he had told her of his love, and though she had accepted it with gentle unresponsiveness he was thrilled by the memory of that last look in her eyes, which had spoken faith, confidence, and perhaps even more. What was that *something* she would tell him if he got Neil safely away? It was to be a reward for his own loyalty — he knew that, by the half fearing tremble of her voice, the sobbing catch of her breath, the strange glow in her eyes. With her brother away would she confide in him? Would she tell him the secret of her slavedom to Strang? Nathaniel was conscious of no madness in the wild hope that filled him; nothing seemed impossible to him now. Marion would meet him at midnight. She would go with him to the boat, and then — ah, he had solved the problem! He would use no force. He would tell her that Neil was in his canoe half a mile out from the shore and that he had promised to leave the island for good if she would go out to bid him good-by. And once there, a half a mile or a mile away, he would tell her that he had lied to her; and he would give her his heart to trample upon to prove the love that had made him do this thing, and then he would row her to the mainland.

It was the sight of Obadiah's cabin that brought his caution back. He came upon it so suddenly that an exclamation of surprise fell unguarded from his lips. There was no light to betray life within. He tried the door and found it locked. He peered in at the windows, listened, and knocked, and at last concealed himself near the path, confident that the little old councilor was still at St. James. For an hour he waited. From the rear of Obadiah's home a narrow footway led toward the lake and Nathaniel followed it, now as warily as an animal in search of prey. For half a mile it took him through the forest and ended at the white sands of the beach. In neither direction could Nathaniel see a light, and keeping close in the shadows of the trees he made his way slowly toward St. James. He had gone but a short distance when he saw a house directly ahead of him, a single gleam of light from a small window telling him that it was inhabited and that its tenants were at home. He circled down close to the water looking for a boat. His heart leaped with sudden exultation when he saw a small skiff drawn upon the beach and his joy was doubled at finding the oars still in the locks. It took him but a moment to shove the light craft into the sea and a minute later he was rowing swiftly away from the land.

Nathaniel was certain that by this time Neil had abandoned his search for the captured *Typhoon* and was probably paddling in the direction of St. James. With the hope of intercepting him he pulled an eighth of a mile from the shore and rowed slowly toward the head of the island. There was no moon, but countless stars glowed in a clear sky and upon the open lake Nathaniel could see for a considerable distance about him. For another hour he rowed back and forth and then beached his boat within a dozen rods of the path that came down from Obadiah's.

It was ten o'clock. Two more hours! He had tried to suppress his excitement, his apprehensions, his eagerness, but now as he went back into the darkness of the forest they burst out anew. What if Marion should not keep the tryst? He thought of the spies whom Neil had said guarded the girl's home — and of Obadiah. Could he trust the old councilor? Should he confide his plot to him and ask his assistance? As the minutes passed and these thoughts recurred again and again in his brain he could not keep the nervousness from growing within him. He was sure now that he would have to fight his battle without Neil. He saw the necessity of coolness, of judgment, and he began to demand these things of himself, struggling sternly against those symptoms of weakness which had replaced his confidence of a short time before. Gradually he fought himself back into his old faith. He would save Marion — without Neil, without Obadiah. If Marion did not come to him by midnight it would be because of the guards against whom Neil had warned him, and he would go to her. In some way he would get her to the boat, even if he had to fight his way through Arbor Croche's men.

With this return of confidence Nathaniel's thoughts reverted to his present greatest need, which was food. Since early morning he had eaten nothing and he began to feel the physical want in a craving that was becoming acutely uncomfortable. If Obadiah had not returned to his home he made up his mind that he would find entrance to the cabin and help himself. A

sudden turn in the path which he was following,
however, revealed one of the councilor's windows
aglow with light, and as he pressed quietly
around the end of the building the sound of a
low voice came to him through the open door.
Cautiously he approached and peered in. A
large oil lamp, the light of which he had seen
in the window, was burning on a table in the
big room but the voice came from the little closet
into which Obadiah had taken him the preceding night. For several minutes he crouched and
listened. He heard the chuckling laugh of the
old councilor — and then an incoherent rav-
ing that set his blood tingling. There is a
horror in the sound of madness, a horror that
creeps to the very pit of one's soul, that sends
shivering dread from every nerve center, that
causes one who is alone with it to sweat with a
nameless fear. It was the voice of madness that
came from that little room. Before it Nathaniel quailed as if a clammy hand had reached out
from the darkness and gripped him by the

throat. He drew back shivering in every limb, and the voice followed him, shrieking now in a sudden burst of insane mirth and dying away a moment later in a hollow cackling laugh that seemed to curdle the blood in his veins. Mad! Obadiah Price was mad! Step by step Nathaniel fell back from the door. He felt himself trembling from head to foot. His heart thumped within his breast like the beating of a hammer. For an instant there was silence — a silence in which strange dread held him breathless while he watched the glow in the door and listened. And after that quiet there came suddenly a cry that ended in the exultant chattering of a name.

At the sound of that name Nathaniel sprang forward again. It was Marion's name and he strained his ears to catch the words that might follow it. As he listened, his head thrust half in at the door, Obadiah's voice became lower and lower, until at last it ceased entirely. Not a step, not a deep breath, not the movement of a hand disturbed the stillness of the little room. By inches Nathaniel drew himself inside the door. His heavy boot caught in a sliver on the step but the rending of wood brought no response. It was the quiet of death that pervaded the cabin, it was a strange, growing fear of death that entered Nathaniel as he now hurried across the room and peered through the narrow aperture. The old councilor was half stretched upon the table, his arms reaching out, his long, thin fingers gripping its edges, his face buried under his shoulders. It looked as if death had come suddenly to him during some terrible convulsion, but after a moment Nathaniel saw that he was breathing. He went over and placed a hand on the old man's twisted back.

" Hello, Obadiah! Hello — hello!" he called cheerfully.

A shudder ran through the councilor's frame, as if the voice had startled him, his arms and body stiffened and slowly he lifted his head. Nathaniel tried to stifle the cry on his lips,

tried to smile — to speak, but the terrible face
that stared up into his own held him silent, motionless. He had heard the voice of madness,
now he looked upon madness in the eyes that
glared at him. In them was no sign of recognition, no passing flash of sanity. The white
face was lined with purplish veins, the mouth
was distorted and the lips bleeding. Involuntarily he stepped back to the end of the table.

At his movement the councilor stretched out
his arms with a sobbing moan.

" Nat — Nat — don't — go —"

He fell again upon his face, clutching the
table in a sudden convulsion. In the next room
Nathaniel had noticed a pail of water and he
brought this and wet the old man's head. For
a long time Obadiah did not move, and when he
did it was to reach out with a groping hand to
find Nathaniel. A change had come into his
face when he lifted it again, the mad fire had
partly burned itself out of his eyes, the old
chuckling laugh came from between his lips.

"A little weakness, Nat — a little weakness," he gasped faintly. "I have it now and then. Excitement — great excitement —" He straightened himself for a moment and stood, swaying free from the table, then collapsed into a chair his head dropping upon his breast.

Without arousing him from the stupor into which he had fallen, Nathaniel again concealed himself in the shadows outside the cabin where he could better guard himself against the possible approach of Mormon visitors. But he did not remain long. He struck a match and saw that it was nearly eleven and a sudden resolution turned him back to the cabin door. He believed that Obadiah would not easily arouse himself from the strange stupor into which he had fallen. Meanwhile he would find food and then conceal himself near the path to intercept Marion.

As he mounted the step he heard for the second time since landing upon the island the solemn tolling of the great bell at St. James, and

as he paused for an instant to listen, peal upon
peal followed the first until its brazen thunder
rolled in one long booming echo through the
forests of the Mormon kingdom. There came a
shrill cry at his back and he whirled about to
see the councilor standing in the center of the
big room, his arms outstretched, his face lifted
as it had been raised in prayer at the tolling of
that same bell the night before — but this time
it was not prayer that fell from his lips.

"Nat, ye have returned in the hour of vengeance! The hand of God is descending upon
the Mormon kingdom!"

His words came in a gasping, but triumphant
cry.

"And to-morrow — to-morrow —" He
stepped forward, his voice crooning a wild joy,
"To-morrow — I — shall — be — king!"

As he spoke the cabin trembled, a tremor
passed under them, and the tolling of the bell
was lost in a sudden tumult that came like the
bursting crash of low thunder.

THE HOUR OF VENGEANCE

" What is it? " cried Nathaniel. He leaped into the room and caught Obadiah by the arm. " What is it? "

" The hand of God! " whispered the old man again. " Nat — Nat —" It was his old self that stood grimacing and twisting his hands before Nathaniel now. " Nat — a thousand armed men are off the coast! The Lamanites of the mainland are descending upon the Mormon kingdom as the hosts of Israel upon Canaan! Strang is doomed — doomed — doomed — and to-morrow I shall be king! " His voice rose in a wailing shriek. He darted to the door and his cackling laugh rang with the old madness as he pointed into the north where a lurid glow had mounted high into the sky.

" The signal fire — the bell! " he gurgled chokingly. " They are calling the Mormons to arms — but it is too late — too late! Ho, ho, it is too late, Nat — too late! " He staggered back, gripping his throat, and fell upon the floor. " Too late — too late," he moaned, groveling weakly, as if struggling for breath. "Too late — Nat — Marion —"

A shiver passed through his body and he lay quite still.

CHAPTER VIII

THE SIX CASTLE CHAMBERS

In an instant Nathaniel was upon his knees beside the prostrate form of the old councilor.

Obadiah's eyes were open, but unseeing; his face was blanched to the whiteness of paper; an almost imperceptible movement of his chest showed that he still breathed. Nathaniel lifted one of the limp hands and its clammy chill struck horror to his heart. Tenderly he lifted the old man and carried him to the cot at the end of the room. He loosened his clothes, tore off the low collar about his throat, and felt with his hand to measure the faint beating of life in the councilor's breast. For a few moments it seemed to grow fainter and fainter, and a choking lump rose in his throat as he watched the pallor of death fixing itself on the councilor's

181

shriveled face. What strange chord of sympathy was it that bound him to this old man? Was it the same mysterious influence that had attracted Marion to him? He dropped upon his knees and called the girl's name softly but it awakened no response in the sightless eyes, no tremor in the parted, unquivering lips. Very slowly as the minutes passed there came a reaction. The pulsations of the weakened heart became a little stronger, he could catch faintly the sound of breath coming from between the old man's lips.

With a gasp of relief Nathaniel rose to his feet. Through the door he saw the red glare growing in the northern sky and heard the great bell at St. James ring a wilder and more excited alarm. For a few moments he stood in silent, listening inaction, his nerves tingling with a strange sensation of impending peril. Obadiah's madness, the mysterious trembling of the earth beneath his feet, the volcano of fire, the clanging of the bell and the councilor's insane rejoicing had all come so suddenly that he was dazed. What great calamity, what fearful vengeance, was about to come upon the Mormon kingdom? Was it possible that the fishermen and settlers of the mainland had risen, as Obadiah had said, and were already at hand to destroy Strang and his people? The thought spurred him to the door. The blood rushed like fire through his veins. What would it mean to Marion — to Neil?

In his excitement he started down the path that led to the lilac hidden home beyond the forest. Then he thought again of Obadiah and his last choking utterance of Marion's name. He had tried to speak of her, even with that death-like rattling of the breath in his throat; and the memory of the old councilor's frantic struggle for words brought Nathaniel quickly back to the cabin. He bent over Obadiah's shriveled form and spoke the girl's name again and again in his ears. There came no response, no quiver of life to show that the old man was conscious of his presence. As he worked over him, bathing his face and chest in cool water, the feeling became strong in him that he was fighting death in this gloomy room for Marion's sake. It was like the whispering of an invisible spirit in his ears — something more than presentiment, something that made his own heart grow faint when death seemed winning in the struggle. His watchfulness was acute, intense, desperate. When, after a time, he straightened himself again, rewarded by Obadiah's more regular breathing, the sweat stood in beads upon his face. He knew that he had triumphed. Obadiah would live, and Marion —

He placed his mouth close to the councilor's ear.

"Tell me about Marion," he said again. "Marion — Marion — Marion —"

He waited, stilling his own breath to catch the sound of a whisper. None came. As he bent over him he saw through the open door that the red glare of fire had faded to a burnt out glow in the sky. In the deep silence the sullen beating of the bell seemed nearer, and he could hear the excited barking of dogs in St. James. Slowly the hope that Obadiah might speak to him died away and he returned to the door. It still lacked an hour of midnight, when Marion had promised to come to him. He was wildly impatient and to his impatience was added the fear that had filled him as he hovered over Obadiah, a nameless, intangible fear — something which he could not have analyzed and which clutched at his heart and urged him to follow the path that led to Marion's. For a time he resisted the impulse. What if she should come by another path while he was gone? He waited nervously in the edge of the forest, watching, and listening for footsteps. Each minute seemed like an hour marked into seconds by the solemn steady tolling of the bell, and after a little he found himself unconsciously measuring time by counting the strokes. Then he went out into the path. He followed it, step by step, until he could no longer see the light in the cabin; his pulse beat a little faster; he stared ahead into the deep gloom between the walls of forest — and quickened his pace. If Marion was coming to him he would meet her. If she was not coming —

In his old fearless way he promptly made up his mind. He would go boldly to the cabin and tell her that Neil was waiting. He felt sure that the alarm sounding from St. James had drawn away the guards and that there would be nothing to interfere with his plan. If she had already left the cabin he would return quickly to Obadiah's. In his eagerness he began to run. Once a sound stopped him — the distant beating of galloping hoofs. He heard the shout of a man, a reply farther away, the quick, excited yelping of a dog. His blood danced as he thought of the gathering of the Mormon fighters, the men and boys racing down the black trails from the inland forests, the excitement in St. James. As he ran on again he thought of

Arbor Croche mustering the panting, vengeful defenders; of Strang, his great voice booming encouragement and promise, above the brazen thunder of the bell; he saw in fancy the frightened huddling groups of women and children and beyond and above all the coming of the " vengeance of God "— a hundred beats, a thousand men — and there went out from his soul if not from his lips a great cry of joy. At the edge of the forest he stopped for a moment. Over beyond the clearing a light burned dimly through the lilacs. The sweet odor of the flowers came to him gently, persuasively, and nerved him into the open. He passed across the open space swiftly and plunged into a tangle of bushes close to the lighted window.

He heard a man's voice within, and then a woman's. Was it Marion? Cautiously Nathaniel crept close to the log wall of the cabin. He reached out, and hesitated. Should he look — as he had done at the king's window? The man's voice came to him again, harsh and angry, and this time it was not a woman's words that he heard but a woman's sobbing cry. He parted the bushes and a glare of light fell on his face. The lamp was on a table and beside the table there sat a woman, her white head turned from him, her face buried in her hands. She was an old woman and he knew that it was Marion's mother. He could not see the man.

Where was Marion? He wormed himself back out of the bushes and walked quickly around the house. There was no other light, no other sign of life except in that one room. With sudden resolution he stepped to the door and knocked loudly.

For a full half minute there was silence, and he knocked again. He heard the approach of a shuffling step, the thump, thump, thump of a cane, and the door swung back. It was the man who opened it, a tall giant of an old man, doubled as if with rheumatism, and close behind him was the frightened face of the woman. An involuntary shudder passed through Nathaniel as he looked at them. They were old — so old that the man's shriveled hands were like those of a skeleton; his giant frame seemed about to totter into ruin, his eyes were sunken until his face gave the horror of a death mask. Was it possible that these people were the father and mother of Marion — and of Neil? As he stepped to the threshold they timidly drew back from him. In a single glance Nathaniel swept the room and what he saw thrilled him, for everywhere were signs of Marion; in the pictures on the walls, the snowy curtains, the cushions in the window-seat — and the huge vase of lilacs on the mantle.

" I am a messenger of the king," he said, advancing and closing the door behind him. " I want to speak with Marion."

" Strang — the king! " cried the old man, clutching the knob of his cane with both hands. " She has gone! "

" Gone! " exclaimed Nathaniel. For an instant his heart bounded with delight. Marion was on her way to the tryst! He sprang back to the door. "When? When did she go?"

The woman had come forward, her hands trembling, her lips quivering. Something in the terror of her face sent the hot blood from Nathaniel's cheeks.

"They sent for her an hour ago," she said. "The king sent Obadiah Price for her! O, my God!" she shrieked suddenly, clutching at her breast, "Tell me — what are they doing with Marion —"

"Shut up!" snarled the old man. "That is Strang's business. She has gone to Strang." With an effort he straightened himself until his towering form rose half a head above Nathaniel. "She has gone to the king," he repeated. "Tell Strang that she will wive him to-night, as she has promised!"

In spite of his effort to control himself a terrible cry burst from Nathaniel's lips. He flung open the door and stood for an instant with his white face turned back.

" She went to the castle — an hour ago? " he cried.

" Yes, to the castle — with Obadiah Price —"

The last words followed him as he sped out into the night. As swiftly as a wolf he raced across the clearing to the trail that led down to St. James. Something seemed to have burst in his brain; something that was not blood, but fire, seemed to burn in his veins — a mad desire to reach Strang, to grip him by the throat, to mete out to him the vengeance of a fiend instead of that of a man. He was too late to save Marion! His brain reeled with the thought. Too late — too late — too late. He panted the words. They came with every gasp for breath. Too late! Too late! His heart pumped like an engine as he strained to keep up his speed. He passed a man and a boy hurrying with their rifles to St. James and made no answer to their shout; a galloping horse forged ahead of him and he tried to keep up with it; and then, at the top of the long hill that sloped down to the stronghold of the Mormon kingdom something seemed to sweep his legs from under him, and he fell panting on the ground. For a few moments he lay there looking down upon the city. The great bell at the temple was now silent. He saw huge fires burning for a mile along the coast, hundreds of lights were twinkling in the harbor, there came up to him softly, subdued by distance, the sound of commotion and excitement far below.

His eyes rested on the beacon above the prophet's home, burning like a ball of fire over the black canopy of tree-tops. Marion was there! He rose to his feet again and went on, reason and judgment returning to him — telling him that he was about to play against odds; that his work was to be one of strength and generalship and not of madness. As he picked his way more slowly and cautiously down the slope a new hope flashed upon him. Was it possible that the discovery of the approach of the main-landers had served to save Marion? In the excitement that followed the calling of the Mormons to arms and the preparations for the defense would Strang, the master of the kingdom, the bulwark of his people, waste priceless time in carrying out the purpose for which he had sent for Marion? Hardly did hope burn anew in his breast when there came another thought to quench it. Why had the king sent for Marion on this particular night and at this late hour? Why, unless at the approach of his enemies he had feared that he might lose his beautiful victim, and in his overmastering passion had called her to him even as his people assembled in defense of his kingdom.

There was desperate coolness in Nathaniel's approach now. Whatever had happened he would do what Neil had threatened to do — kill Strang. And whatever had happened he would take Marion away with him if it was only her dead body that he carried in his arms. To do these things he needed strength. He advanced more slowly and drew deeper and deeper drafts of air into his exhausted lungs. At the edge of the grove surrounding the castle he paused to listen. For the first time it occurred to Nathaniel that the prophet might have assembled some of his fighters to the defense of his harem, which he knew would be one of the first places to feel the vengeance of the outraged men of the mainland. But he heard no voices ahead of him. There were no fires to betray the approach of the enemy. Not even the barking of a dog gave warning of his stealthy advance. Soon he could make out a light in the king's house. A few steps more and he saw that the door was open, as it had been on his first visit to the castle. He dodged swiftly from bush to bush, darted under the window through which he had seen Marion, leaped lightly up the broad steps and sprang into the great room, his pistol cocked in his hand.

The room was empty. He listened, but not a sound came to his ears except the rustling of a curtain in the breeze. The hugh lamp over

194

the table was burning dimly. The five doors leading from the room were tightly closed. Nathaniel held his breath, tried to still the tumultuous pounding of his heart as he waited for a sound of life — a step beyond those doors, a woman's voice, a child's cry. But none came. The stillness of desertion hovered about him. He went to one of the five doors. It was not locked. He opened it silently, with the caution of a thief, and there loomed before him a chaos of gloom.

"Hello!" he called gently. "Hello — Hello —"

There was no answer. He struck a match and advanced step by step, holding the yellow bit of flame above his head. It disclosed the narrow walls of a hall and an open door leading into another room. The match sputtered and went out and he lighted another. On a little table just outside the door was a half burned candle and he replaced his match with this. Then he went in.

At a glance he knew that he had entered a woman's room, redolent with the perfume of flowers. On one side was a bed and close beside it a cradle with a child's toys scattered about it. The tumbled coverlets showed that both had been recently used. About the room were thrown articles of wearing apparel; a trunk had been dragged from a closet and was half packed; everywhere was the disorder of hurried flight. For a few moments the depth of his despair held Nathaniel motionless. The castle was deserted — Marion was gone! He ran back into the great room, no longer trying to still the sound of his footsteps, and opened a second door. The same silence greeted him, the same disorder, the same evidence that the wives and children of the Mormon king had fled. He went into a third room — and then a fourth.

For an instant he paused at the threshold of this fourth chamber. A light was burning in the room at the end of the hall. The door was closed with the exception of an inch or two.

" Marion ! " he called softly, and listened intently.

He went on when there was no reply, and pushed open the door.

A candle was burning on a stand in front of a mirror. The room was as empty as the others. But there was no disorder here. The bed was unused, the garments in the open closet had not been disarranged. On the floor beside the bed was a pair of shoes and as Nathaniel saw them his heart seemed to leap to his throat and stifled the cry that was on his lips. He took one of them in his hand, his whole being throbbing with excitement. It was Marion's shoe — encrusted with mud and torn as he had seen it in the forest. With her name falling from his lips in a pleading cry he now searched the room and on the stand in front of the mirror he found a lilac colored ribbon, soiled and crumpled. It was Marion's ribbon — the one he had seen last in her hair, and he crushed it to his lips as he ran back into the great room, calling out her name again and again in the torture of helplessness that now possessed him.

Mechanically, rather than with reason, he went to the fifth and last door. His candle had become extinguished in his haste and after he had opened the door he stopped at the threshold of the black hall to light it again. There was a moment's pause as he searched his pockets for a match, a silence in which he listened as he searched, and suddenly as he was about to strike the sulphur tipped splint there came to his ears a sound that held him chained to the spot. It was the sobbing of a woman; or was it a child? In a moment he knew that it was a woman; and then the sobbing ceased.

There was nothing but darkness ahead of him; no ray of light shone under the door; the chamber itself was in utter gloom. As quietly as possible he relighted his candle. A glance assured him that this hall was different from the others; it was deeper, and there were two doors at the end of it instead of one. Through which of these doors had come the sound of sobbing he had heard?

He approached and listened. Each moment added to his excitement, his fears, his hopes, but at last he opened the door on the left. The room was empty; there was the same disorder as before; the same signs of hurried flight. It was the room on the right! His heart almost stopped its beating as he placed his hand on the latch, lifted it, and pushed the door in. Kneeling beside the bed he saw a woman. She had turned toward the light and in the dim illumination of the room Nathaniel recognized the beautiful face he had seen at the king's castle the preceding day — the face of the woman who had sent him to find the prophet, who had placed her gentle hand on Marion's head as he had looked through the window. There was no fear in her eyes as she saw Nathaniel. Something more terrible than that shone in their glorious depths as she rose to her feet and stood before him, her face lined with grief, her mouth twitching in agony. She stood with clenched hands, her bosom rising and falling in the passion of the storm within her; and she sobbed even as Nathaniel paused there, unmanned in this sudden presence of a distress greater than his own; sobbed in a choking, tearless way, waiting for him to speak.

"Forgive me," he spoke gently. "I have come — for — Marion." He felt that he had no reason to lie to this woman. His face betrayed his own anguish as he came nearer to her. "I want Marion," he repeated. "My God, won't you tell me —?"

She struggled to calm herself as he spoke the girl's name.

"Marion is not here," she said. She crushed his hands against her bosom and a softer look came into her eyes; her voice was low and sweet, as it had been the morning he asked for Strang. As she saw the despair deepening in the man's face a great pity swept over her and she stretched out her arms to him with an aching cry, " Marion is gone — gone — gone," she moaned, " and you must go, too! O, I know you love her — she told me that you loved her, as I love Strang, my king! We have both lost — lost — and you must go — as — I — shall — go!" She turned away from him with a cry so heart-breaking in its pain that Nathaniel felt himself trembling to the soul. In another instant she had faced him again, fighting back a strange calm into her face.

"I love Marion," she breathed softly. " I would help you — I would help her — if I could." For a moment her pale beautiful face was filled with a light that might have shone from the face of an angel. " Don't you understand?" she continued, scarcely above a whisper. " I have been Strang's one great love — his life — until Marion came into his heart. I have lost — you have lost — but mine is the more bitter because Marion loves you, and Strang —"

With a cry Nathaniel sprang to her side.

201

The candle fell from his hand, sputtered on the floor, and left them in darkness.

"Marion loves me! You say that Marion loves me?"

The woman's voice came to him in a whisper filled with the sweetness of sympathy.

"She said so to-night — in this room. She told me that she loved you as she never thought that she could love a man in this world. O, my God, is that not a balm for your heart, if it is broken? And Strang — my Strang — has forgotten his love for me!"

Nathaniel reached out his arms. They found the woman and for a time he held her hands in his, while a great silence fell upon them. He could hear the sobbing of her breath and as her fingers tightened about his own his heart seemed bursting with its hatred of this man who called himself a prophet of God; a hatred that burned furiously even as his being throbbed with the wild joy of the words he had just heard.

"Where is Marion?" he pleaded.

" I don't know," replied the woman. " They took her away alone. The others have gone to the temple."

" Do you think she is at the temple? " he inquired insistently.

" No. One of the others came back a little while ago. She said that Marion was not there."

" Where is Strang? "

This time he felt the woman tremble.

" Strang —"

She drew her hands away from him. There was a strange quiver in her voice.

" Yes — where is Strang? "

There came no reply.

" Tell me — where is he? "

" I don't know."

" Is he at the temple? "

" I don't know."

He could hear her stifled breath; he could almost feel her trembling, an arm's reach out there in the darkness. What a woman was this whose heart the Mormon king had broken for a new love!

"Listen," he said gently. "I am going to find Marion. I am going to take her away. To-morrow you shall have Strang again — if he is alive!"

There was no answer and he moved slowly back to the door. He closed it after him as he entered the hall. Once in the big room he paused for a moment under the hanging lamp to examine his pistol and then went outside. The grove in which the castle stood was absolutely deserted. So far as he could see not even a guard watched over the property of the king. Nathaniel had become too accustomed to the surprises of Beaver Island to wonder at this. He could see by the lights flaring along the harbor that the castle was in an isolated position and easy of attack. From what Strang's wife had told him and the evidences of panic in the chambers of the harem he believed that the Mormon king had abandoned the castle to its fate and that the approaching conflict would center about the temple.

Was Marion at the temple? If so he realized that she was beyond his reach. But the woman had said that she was not there. Where could she have gone? Why had not Strang taken her with his wives? In a flash Nathaniel thought of Arbor Croche and Obadiah — the two men who always knew what the king was doing. If he could find the sheriff alone — if he could only nurse Obadiah back into sane life again! He thrust his pistol into its holster. There was but one thing for him to do and that was to return to the old councilor. It would be madness for him to go down to St. James. He had lost — Strang had won. But his love for Marion was undying. If he found her Strang's wife it would make no difference to him. It would all be evened up when he killed the king. For Marion loved him — loved him —

He turned his face toward Obadiah's, his heart singing the glad words which the woman had spoken to him back there in the sixth chamber.

And as he was about to take the first step in that long race back to the mad councilor's he heard behind him the approach of quick feet. He crouched behind a clump of bushes and waited. A shadowy form was hurrying through the grove. It passed close to him, mounted the castle steps, and in the doorway turned and looked back for an instant in the direction of St. James.

Nathaniel's lips quivered; the pounding of his heart half choked him; a shriek of mad, terrible joy was ready to leap from his lips.

There in the dim glow of the great lamp stood Strang, the Mormon king.

CHAPTER IX

THE HAND OF FATE

Like a panther Nathaniel crouched and watched the man on the steps. His muscles jerked, his hands were clenched; each instant he seemed about to spring. But he held himself back until Strang had passed through the door. Then he slipped along the log wall of the castle, hugging the shadows, fearing that the king might reappear and see him in time to close the door. What an opportunity fate had made for him! His fingers itched to get at Strang's thick bull-like throat. He felt no fear, no hesitation about the outcome of the struggle with this giant prophet of God. He did not plan to shoot, for a shot would destroy the secret of Marion's fate. He would choke the truth from Strang; rob him of life slowly, gasp by gasp, until in the horror of death the king would reveal her hiding-place — would tell what he had done with her.

Then he would kill him!

There was the strength of tempered steel in his arms; his body, slender as an athlete's, quivered to hurl itself into action. Up the steps he crept so cautiously that he made no sound. In the intensity of his purpose Nathaniel looked only ahead of him — to the door. He did not see that another figure was stealing through the gloom behind him as cautiously, as quietly as himself. He passed through the door and stood erect. Strang had not seen him. He had not heard him. He was standing with his huge back toward him, facing the hall that led to the sixth chamber — and the woman. Nathaniel drew his pistol. He would not shoot, but Strang might be made to tell the truth with death leveling itself at his heart. He groped behind him, found the door, and slammed it shut. There would be no retreat for the king!

And the man who turned toward him at the slamming of that door, turned slowly, coolly, and gazed into the black muzzle of his pistol looked, indeed, every inch of him a king. The muscles of his face betrayed no surprise, no fear. His splendid nerve was unshaken, his eyes unfaltering as they rose above the pistol to the face behind it. For fifteen seconds there was a strange terrible silence as the eyes of the two men met. In that quarter of a minute Nathaniel knew that he had not guessed rightly. Strang was not afraid. He would not tell him where Marion was. The insuperable courage of this man maddened Captain Plum and unconsciously his finger fell upon the trigger of his pistol. He almost shrieked the words that he meant to speak calmly:

"Where is Marion?"

"She is safe, Captain Plum. She is where the friends who are invading us from the mainland will have no chance of finding her."

Strang spoke as quietly as though in his own

office beside the temple. Suddenly he raised his voice.

"She is safe, Captain Plum — safe!"

His eyes wavered, and traveled beyond. As accurately as a striking serpent Nathaniel measured that glance. It had gone to the door. He heard a movement, felt a draft of air, and in an instant he whirled about with his pistol pointed to the door. In another instant he had fired and the huge form of Arbor Croche toppled headlong into the room. A roar like that of a beast came from behind him and before he could turn again Strang was upon him. In that moment he felt that all was lost. Under the weight of the Mormon king he was crushed to the floor; his pistol slipped from his grasp; two great hands choked a despairing cry from his throat. He saw the prophet's face over him, distorted with passion, his huge neck bulging, his eyes flaming like angry garnets. He struggled to free his pinioned arms, to wrench off the death grip at his throat, but his efforts were like

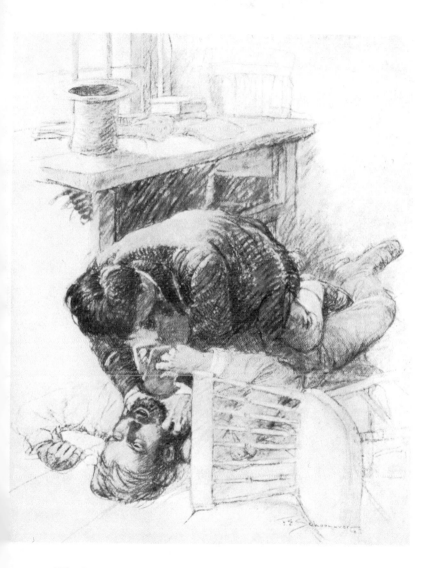

His fingers twined about the purplish throat.—*Page* 211

those of a child against a giant. In a last
terrible attempt he drew up his knees inch by
inch under the weight of his enemy; it was his
only chance — his only hope. Even as he felt
the fingers about his throat sinking like hot iron
into his flesh and the breath slipping from his
body he remembered this murderous knee-punch
of the rough fighters of the inland seas and with
all the life that remained in him he sent it crushing into the abdomen of the Mormon king. It
was a moment before he knew that it had been
successful, before the film cleared from his eyes
and he saw Strang groveling at his feet; another
moment and he had hurled himself on the prophet. His fist shot out like a hammer against
Strang's jaw. Again and again he struck until the great shaggy head fell back limp.
Then his fingers twined themselves like the links
of a chain about the purplish throat and he
choked until Strang's eyes opened wide and life-
less and his convulsions ceased. He would have
held on until there was no doubt of the end, had

not the king's wife — the woman whose misery he had shared that night — suddenly flung herself with a piercing cry, between him and the blackened face, clutching at his hands with all her fragile strength.

" My God, you are killing him — killing him! " she moaned.

Her eyes blazed as she tore at his fingers.

" You are killing him — killing him! " she shrieked. " He has not destroyed Marion! You said you would take her and leave him — for me —" She struck her head against his breast, tearing the flesh of his wrists with her nails.

Nathaniel loosened his grip and staggered to his feet.

" For you! " he panted. " If you had only come — a little sconer —" He stumbled to his pistol and picked it up. " I am afraid he is — dead! "

He did not look back.

Arbor Croche barred the door. He had not moved since he had fallen. His head was

twisted so that his face was turned to the glow
of the lamp and Nathaniel shuddered as he saw
where his shot had struck. He had apparently
died with that last cry on his lips.

There was no longer a fear of the Mormons
in Nathaniel. He believed the king and Arbor
Croche dead, and that in the gloom and excitement of the night he could go among the
people of St. James undiscovered. A great load
was lifted from his soul, for if he had not been
in time to save Marion he had at least delivered
her after a short bondage. He had now only to
find Marion and she would go with him, for she
loved him — and Strang was no more.

He hurried through the grove toward the temple. Even before he had come near to it he
could see that a great crowd had congregated
there. The street which he passed was deserted.
No lights shone in the houses. Even the dogs
were gone. For the first time he understood
what it meant. The whole town had fled to that
huge log stronghold for protection. Buildings

and trees shut out his view seaward but he could see the flare of great fires mounting into the sky and he knew that those who were not at the temple were guarding the shore.

Suddenly he almost fell over a figure in his path. It was an old woman mumbling and sobbing incoherently as she stumbled weakly in the direction of the temple. Like an inspiration the thought came to him that here was his opportunity of gaining admittance to that multitude of women and children. He seized the old woman by the arm and spoke words of courage to her as he half carried her on her way. A few minutes more and a blaze of light burst upon them and the great square in which the temple was situated lay open before them. Half a hundred yards ahead a fire was burning; oil and pine sent their lurid flame high up into the night, and in the thick gloom behind it, intensified by the blinding glare, Nathaniel saw the shadows of men. He caught the old woman in his arms and went on boldly. He passed close to a thin

214

line of waiting men, saw the faint glint of firelight on their rifles, and staggering past them
unchallenged with his weight he stopped for a
moment to look back.   The effect was startling.
Beyond the three great fires that blazed around
the temple the clearing was bathed in a sea of
light; in its concealment of giant trees the temple was buried in gloom.   From the gloom a
hundred cool men might slaughter five times
their number charging across that illumined
death-square!

Nathaniel could not repress a shudder as he
looked.   Screened behind each of the three fires
was a cannon.   He figured that there were more
than a hundred rifles in that silent cordon of
men.   What was there on the opposite side of
the temple?

He turned with the old woman and joined
the throng that was seething about the temple
doors.   There were women, children and old men,
crushing and crowding, fighting with panic-
stricken fierceness for admittance to the thick log

walls. Through the doors there came the low thunder of countless voices pierced by the shrill cries of little children. Foot by foot Nathaniel fought his way up the steps. At the top were drawn a dozen men forming barriers with their rifles. One of them shoved him back.

"Not you!" he shouted. "This is for the women!"

Nathaniel fell back, filled with horror. A glance had shown him the vast dimly lighted interior of the temple packed to suffocation. What sins had this people wrought that it thus feared the vengeance of the men from the mainland! He felt the sweat break out upon his face as he thought of Marion being in that mob, tired and fainting with her terrible day's experience — perhaps dying under the panic-stricken feet of those stronger than herself. He hoped now for that which at first had filled him with despair — that Strang had hidden Marion away from the terror and suffocation of this multitude that fought for its breath within the temple. Freeing himself of the crowd he ran to the farther side of the building. A fourth fire blazed in his face. But on this side there was no cannon; scarcely a score of men were guarding the rear of the temple.

For a full minute he stood concealed in the gloom. He realized now that it would be useless to return to Obadiah. The old councilor could probably have told him all that he had discovered for himself; that Marion had gone to the castle — that Strang intended to make her his bride that night. But did Obadiah know that the castle had been abandoned? Did he know that the king's wives had sought refuge in the temple, and did he know where Marion was hidden? Nathaniel could assure himself but one answer; Obadiah, struck down by his strange madness, was more ignorant than he himself of what had occurred at St. James.

While he paused a heavy noise arose that quickened his heart-beats and sent the blood through his veins in wild excitement. From far down by the shore there came the roar of a cannon. It was closely followed by a second and a third, and hardly was the night shaken by their thunder than a mighty cheering of men swept up from the fire-rimmed coast. The battle had begun! Nathaniel leaped out into the glow of the great blazing fire beyond the temple; he heard a warning shout as he darted past the men; for an instant he saw their white faces staring at him from the firelight — heard a second shout, which he knew was a command — and was gone. Half a dozen rifles cracked behind him and a yell of joyful defiance burst from his throat as the bullets hissed over his head. The battle had begun! Another hour and the Mormon kingdom would be at the mercy of the avenging host from the mainland — and Marion would be his own for ever! He heard again the deep rumble of a heavy gun and from its sullen detonation he knew that it was fired from a ship at sea. A nearer crash of returning fire turned him into a deserted street down which he ran wildly, on past the last houses of the town, until he came to the foot of a hill up which he climbed more slowly, panting like a winded animal.

From its top he could look down upon the scene of battle. To the eastward stretched the harbor line with its rim of fires. A glance showed him that the fight was not to center about these. They had served their purpose, had forced the mainlanders to seek a landing farther down the coast. The light of dawn had already begun to disperse the thick gloom of night and an eighth of a mile below Nathaniel the Mormon forces were creeping slowly along the shore. The pale ghostly mistiness of the sea hung like a curtain between him and what was beyond, and even as he strained his eyes to catch a glimpse of the avenging fleet a vivid light leaped out of the white distance, followed by the thunder of a cannon. He saw the head of the Mormon line falter. In an instant it had been thrown into confusion. A second shot from the sea — a storm of cheering voices from out of that white chaos of mist — and the Mormons fell back from the shore in a panic-stricken, fleeing mob. Were those frightened cowards the fierce fighters of whom he had heard so much? Were they the men who had made themselves masters of a kingdom in the land of their enemies — whose mere name carried terror for a hundred miles along the coast? He was stupefied, bewildered. He made no effort to conceal himself as they approached the hill, but drew his pistol, ready to fire down upon them as they came. Suddenly there was a change. So quickly that he could scarcely believe his eyes the flying Mormons had disappeared. Not a man was visible upon that narrow plain between the hill and the sea. Like a huge covey of quail they had dropped to the ground, their rifles lost in that ghostly gloom through which the voices of the mainlanders came in fierce cries of triumph. It was magnificent! Even as the crushing truth of what it all meant came to him, the fighting blood in his veins leaped at the sight of it — the pretended effect of the shots from sea, the sham confusion, the disorderly flight, the wonderful quickness and precision with which the rabble of armed men had thrown itself into ambush!

Would the mainlanders rush into the trap? Had some keen eye seen those shadowy forms dropping through the mist? Each instant the ghostly pall that shut out vision seaward seemed drifting away. Nathaniel's staring eyes saw a vague shape appear in it, an indistinct dirt-gray blotch, and he knew that it was a boat. Another followed, and then another; he heard the sound of oars, the grinding of keels upon the sand, and where the Mormons had been a few moments before the beach was now alive with mainlanders. In the growing light he could make out the king's men below him, inanimate spots in the middle of the narrow plain. Helpless he stood clutching his pistol, the horror in him growing with each breath. Could he give no warning? Could he do nothing — nothing —

At least he could join in the fight! He ran down the hill, swinging to the left of the Mormons. Half way, and he stopped as a thundering cheer swept up from the shore. The mainlanders had started toward the hill! Without rank, without order — shouting their triumph as they came they were rushing blindly into the arms of the ambush! A shriek of warning left Nathaniel's lips. It was drowned in a crash of rifle fire. Volley after volley burst from that shadowy stretch of plain. Before the furious fire the van of the mainlanders crumpled into ruin. Like chaff before a wind those behind were swept back. Apparently they were flying without waiting to fire a shot! Nathaniel dashed down into the plain. Ahead of him the Mormons were charging in a solid line, and in another moment the shore had become a mass of fighting men. Far to the left he saw a group of the mainlanders running along the beach toward the conflict. If he could only intercept them — and bring them into the rear! Like the wind he sped to cut them off, shouting and firing his pistol.

He won by a hundred yards and stood panting as they came toward him. Dawn had dispelled the mist-gloom and as the mainlanders drew nearer he discerned in their lead a figure that brought a cry of joy from his lips.

" Neil! " he shouted. " Neil —"

He turned as Marion's brother darted to his side.

" This way — from behind! "

The two led the way, side by side, followed by a dozen men. A glance told Nathaniel that nothing much less than a miracle could turn the tide of battle. Half of the mainlanders were fighting in the water. Others were struggling desperately to get away in the boats. Foot by foot the Mormons were crushing them back, their battle cries now turned into demoniac yells of victory. Into the rear of the struggling mass, firing as they ran, charged the handful of men behind Captain Plum and Neil. For a little space the king's men gave way before them and with wild cheers the powerful fishermen from the coast fought their way toward their comrades. Many of them were armed with long knives; some had pistols; others used their empty rifles as clubs. A dozen more men and they would have split like a wedge through the Mormon mass. Above the din of battle Nathaniel's voice rose in thundering shouts to the men in the sea, and close beside him he heard Neil shrieking out a name between his blows. Like demons they fought straight ahead, slashing with their knives. The Mormon line was thinning. The mainlanders had turned and were fighting their way back, gaining foot by foot what they had lost. Suddenly there came a terrific cheer from the plain and the hope that had flamed in Nathaniel's breast died out as he heard it. He knew what it meant — that the Mormons at St. James had come to reinforce their comrades. He fought now to reach the boats, calling to Neil, whom he could no longer see. Even in that moment he thought of Marion. His only chance was to escape with the others, his only hope of wresting her from the kingdom lay in his own freedom. He had waited too long. A crushing blow fell upon him from behind and with a last cry to Neil he sank under the trampling feet. Indistinctly there came to him the surging shock of the fresh body of Mormons. The din about him became fainter and fainter as though he was being carried rapidly away from it; shouting voices came to him in whispers, and deadened sounds, like the quick tapping of a finger on his forehead, were all that he heard of the steady rifle fire that pursued the defeated mainlanders in their flight.

After a little he began struggling back into consciousness. There was a splitting pain somewhere in his head and he tried to reach his hand to it.

" You won't have to carry him," he heard a voice say. " Give him a little water and he'll walk."

He felt the dash of the water in his face and it put new life into him. Somebody had raised him to a sitting posture and was supporting him there while a second person bound a cloth about his head. He opened his eyes and the light of day shot into them like a stinging, burning charge of needle-points, and he closed them again with a sharp cry of pain. That second's glance had shown him that it was a woman who was binding his head. He had not seen her face. Beyond her he had caught a half formed vision of many people and the glistening edge of the sea, and as he lay with closed eyes the murmur of voices came to him. The support at his back was taken away, slowly, as if the person who held him feared that he would. fall. Nathaniel stiffened himself to show his returning strength and opened his eyes again. This time the pain was not so great. A few yards away he saw a group of people and among them were women; still farther away, so far that his brain grew dizzy as he looked, there was a black moving crowd. He was among the wounded. The Mormon women were here. Down there along the shore — among the dead — had assembled the population of St. James.

A strange sickness overpowered him and he sank back against his supporter. A cool hand passed over his face. It was a soothing, gentle touch — the hand of the woman. He felt the sweep of soft hair against his cheek — a breath whispering in his ear.

" You will be better soon."

His heart stood still.

" You will be better —"

Against his rough cheek there fell the soft pressure of a woman's lips.

Nathaniel pulled himself erect, every drop of blood in him striving for the mastery of his body, his vision, his strength. He tried to turn, but strong arms seized him from behind. A man's voice spoke to him, a man's strength held him. In an agony of appeal Marion's name burst from his lips.

" Sh-h-!" warned the voice behind him. " Are you crazy? "

The arms relaxed their hold and Nathaniel dragged himself to his knees. The woman was gone. As far as he could see there were people — scores of them, hundreds of them — multiplied into thousands and millions as he looked, until there was only a black cloud about him. He staggered to his feet and a strong hand kept him from falling while his brain slowly cleared. The millions and thousands and hundreds of people dissolved themselves into the day until only a handful was left where he had seen multitudes. He turned his face weakly to the man beside him.

" Where did she go? " he asked.

It was a boyish face into which his pleading eyes gazed, a face white with the strain of battle, reddened a little on one cheek with a smear of blood, and there was a startled, frightened look in it that did not come of the strife that had passed.

" Who? What are you talking about? "

" The woman," whispered Nathaniel. " The woman — Marion — who kissed — me —"

The young fellow's hand gripped his arm in a sudden fierce clutch.

" You've been dreaming! " he exclaimed in a threatening voice. " Shut up! " He spoke the words loudly. Then quickly dropping his voice to a whisper he added, " For God's sake don't betray her! They saw her with us — everybody knows that it was the king's wife with you! "

The king's wife! Nathaniel was too weak to analyze the words beyond the fact that they carried the dread truth of his fears deep into his soul. Who would have come to him but Marion? Who else would have kissed him? It was her voice that had whispered in his ear — the thrill of her hand that had passed over his face. And this man had said that she was the wife of the king! He heard the voices of other men near him but did not understand what they were saying. He knew that after a moment there was a man on each side of him holding him by the arms, and mechanically he moved his legs, knowing that they wanted him to walk. They did not guess how weak he was — how he struggled to keep from becoming too great a weight on their hands. Once or twice they stopped in their agonizing climb up the hill. On its top the cool sea air swept into Nathaniel's face and it was like water to a parched throat.

After a time — it seemed a day of terrible work and pain to him — they came to the streets of the town, and in a half conscious sort of way he cursed at the rabble trailing at their heels. They passed close to the temple, dirt and blood and a burning torment shutting the vision of it from his eyes, and beyond this there was another crowd. An aisle opened for them, as it had opened for others ahead of them. In front of the jail they stopped. Nathaniel's head hung heavily upon his breast and he made no effort to raise it. All ambition and desire had left him, all desire but one, and that was to drop upon the ground and lie there for endless, restful years. What consciousness was left in him was ebbing swiftly; he saw black, fathomless night about him and the earth seemed slipping from under his feet.

A voice dragged him back into life — a voice that boomed in his ears like rolling thunder and set every fiber in him quivering with emotion. He drew himself erect with the involuntary strength of one mastering the last spasm of death and as they dragged him through the door he saw there within an arm's reach of him the great, living face of Strang, gloating at him as if from out of a mist — red eyed, white fanged, filled with the vengefulness of a beast.

The great voice rumbled in his ears again.

"Take that man to the dungeon!"

CHAPTER X

THE voice — the condemning words — followed Nathaniel as he staggered on between his two guards; it haunted him still as the cold chill of the rotting dungeon walls struck in his face; it remained with him as he stood swaying alone in the thick gloom — the voice rumbling in his ears, the words beating against his brain until the shock of them sickened him, until he stretched out his arms and there fell from him such a cry as had never tortured his lips before.

Strang was alive! He had left the spark of life in him, and the woman who loved him had fanned it back into full flame.

Strang was alive! And Marion — Marion was his wife!

The voice of the king taunted him from the black chaos that hid the dungeon walls. The words struck at him, filling his head with shooting pain, and he tottered back and sank to the ground to get away from them. They followed, and that vengeful leer of the king was behind them, urging them on, until they beat his face into the sticky earth, and smothered him into what he thought was death.

There came rest after that, a long silent rest. When Nathaniel slowly climbed up out of the ebon shadows again the first consciousness that came to him was that the word-demons had stopped their beating against his brain and that he no longer heard the voice of the king. His relief was so great that he breathed a restful sigh. Something touched him then. Great God! were they coming back? Were they still there — waiting — waiting —

It was a wonderfully familiar voice that spoke to him.

" Hello there, Nat! Want a drink? "

He gulped eagerly at the cool liquid that touched his lips.

" Neil," he whispered.

" It's me, Nat. They chucked me in with you. Hell's hole, isn't it? "

Nathaniel sat up, Neil's strong arm at his back. There was a light in the room now and he could see his companion's face, smiling at him encouragingly. The sight of it was like an elixir to him. He drank again and new life coursed through him.

" Yes — hell of a hole! " he repeated drowsily. " Sorry for you — Neil —" and he seemed to sleep again.

Neil laughed as he wiped his companion's face with a wet cloth.

" I'm used to it, Nat. Been here before," he said. " Can you get up? There's a bench over here — not long enough to stretch you out on or I would have made you a bed of it, but it's better than this mud to sit on."

He put his arms about Nathaniel and helped

him to his feet. For a few moments the wounded man stood without moving.

" I'm not very bad, I guess," he said, taking a slow step. " Where is the seat, Neil? I'm going to walk to it. What sort of a bump have I got on the head?"

" Nothing much," assured Neil. " Suspicious, though," he grinned cheerfully. " Looks as though you were running and somebody came up and tapped you from behind! "

Nathaniel's strength returned to him quickly. The pain had gone from his head and his eyes no longer hurt him. In the dim candle-light he could distinguish the four walls of the dungeon, glistening with the water and mold that reeked from between their rotting logs. The floor was of wet, sticky earth which clung to his boots, and the air that he breathed filled his nostrils and throat with the uncomfortable thickness of a night fog at sea. Through it the candle burned in a misty halo. Near the candle, which stood on a shelf-like table against one of the walls, was a big dish which caught Nathaniel's eyes.

" What's that? " he asked pointing toward it.

" Grub," replied Neil. " Hungry? "

He went to the table and got the plate of food. There were chunks of boiled meat, unbuttered bread, and cold potatoes. For several minutes they ate in silence. Now that Nathaniel was himself again Neil could no longer keep up his forced spirits. Both realized that they had played their game and that it had ended in defeat. And each believed that it was in his individual power to alleviate to some extent the other's misery. To Neil what was ahead of them held no mystery. A few hours more and then — death. It was only the form in which it would come that troubled him, that made him think. Usually the victims of this dungeon cell were shot. Sometimes they were hanged. But why tell Nathaniel? So he ate his meat and bread without words, waiting for the other to speak, as the other waited for him. And Nathaniel, on his part, kept to himself the secret of Marion's fate. After they had done with the meat and the bread and the cold potatoes he pulled out his beloved pipe and filled it with the last scraps of his tobacco, and as the fumes of it clouded round his head, soothing him in its old friendship, he told of his fight with Strang and his killing of Arbor Croche.

"I'm glad for Winnsome's sake," said Neil, after a moment. "Oh, if you'd only killed Strang!"

Nathaniel thought of what Marion had said to him in the forest.

"Neil," he said quietly, "do you know that Winnsome loves you — not as the little girl whom you toted about on your shoulders — but as a woman? Do you know that?" In the other's silence he added, "When I last saw Marion she sent this message to you — ' Tell Neil that he must go, for Winnsome's sake. Tell him that her fate is shortly to be as cruel as mine — tell him that Winnsome loves him and that she will escape and come to him on the mainland.' " Like words of fire they had burned themselves in his brain and as Nathaniel repeated them he thought of that other broken heart that had sobbed out its anguish to him in the castle chamber. " Neil, a man can die easier when he knows that a woman loves him! "

He had risen to his feet and was walking back and forth through the thick gloom.

" I'm glad! " Neil's voice came to him softly, as though he scarcely dared to speak the words aloud. After a moment he added, " Have you got a pencil, Nat? I would like to leave a little note for Winnsome."

Nathaniel found both pencil and paper in one of his pockets and Neil dropped upon his knees in the mud beside the table. Ten minutes later he turned to Nathaniel and a great change had come into his face.

" She always seemed like such a little child to me that I never dared — to — tell her," he faltered. " I've done it in this."

" How will you get the note to her? "

" I know the jailer. Perhaps when he comes to bring us our dinner I can persuade him to send it to her."

Nathaniel thrust his hands into his pockets. His fingers dug into Obadiah's gold.

" Would this help? " he asked.

He brought out a shimmering handful of it and counted the pieces upon the table.

" Two hundred dollars — if he will deliver that note," he said.

Neil stared at him in amazement.

" If he won't take it for that — I've got more. I'll go a thousand! "

Neil stood silent, wondering if his companion was mad. Nathaniel saw the look in his face and his own flushed with sudden excitement.

" Don't you understand? " he cried. " That note means Heaven or hell for Winnsome — it means life — her whole future! And you know what this cell means for us," he said more calmly. " It means that we're at the end of our rope, that the game is up, that neither of us will ever see Marion or Winnsome again. That note is the last word in life from us — from you. It's a dying prayer. Tell Winnsome your love, tell her that it is your last wish that she go out into the big, free world — away from this hell-hole, away from Strang, away from the Mormons, and live as other women live! And commanded by your love — she will go!"

"I've told her that!" breathed Neil.

"I knew you would!"

Nathaniel threw another handful of gold on the table.

"Five hundred!" he exclaimed. "It's cheap enough for a woman's soul!"

He motioned for Neil to put the money in his pocket. The pain was coming back into his head, he grew dizzy, and hastened to the bench. Neil came and sat beside him.

"So you think it's the end?" he asked. He was glad that his companion had guessed the truth.

" Don't you? "

" Yes."

There was a minute's dark silence. The ticking of Nathaniel's watch sounded like the tapping of a stick.

" What will happen? "

" I don't know. But whatever it may be it will come to us soon. Usually it happens at night."

" There is no hope? "

" Absolutely none. The whole mainland is at the mercy of Strang. He fears no retribution now, no punishment for his crimes, no hand stronger than his own. He will not even give us the pretense of a hearing. I am a traitor, a revolutionist — you have attempted the life of the king. We are both condemned — both doomed."

Neil spoke calmly and his companion strove to master the terrible pain at his heart as he thought of Marion. If Neil could go to the end like a martyr he would at least make an attempt to do as much. Yet he could not help from saying:

" What will become of Marion? "

He felt the tremor that passed through his companion's body.

" I have implored Winnsome to do all that she can to get her away," replied Neil. " If Marion won't go —" He clenched his hands with a moaning curse and sprang to his feet, again pacing back and forth through the gloomy dungeon. " If she won't go I swear that Strang's triumph will be short !" he cried suddenly. " I can not guess the terrible power that the king possesses over her, but I know that once his wife she will not endure it long. The moment she becomes that, her bondage is broken. I know it. I have seen it in her eyes. She will kill herself ! "

Nathaniel rose slowly from the bench and came to his side.

" She won't do that ! " he groaned. " My God — she won't do that ! "

Neil's face was blanched to the whiteness of paper.

" She will," he repeated quietly. " Her terrible pact with Strang will have been fulfilled. And I — I am glad — glad —"

He raised his arms to the dripping blackness of the dungeon ceiling, his voice shaking with a cold, stifled anguish. Nathaniel drew back from that tall, straight figure, step by step, as though to hide beyond the flickering candle glow the betrayal that had come into his face, the blazing fire that seemed burning out his eyes. If what Neil had said was true —

Something choked him as he dropped alone upon the bench.

If it was true — Marion was dead!

He dropped his head in his hands and sat for a long time in silence, listening to Neil as he walked tirelessly over the muddy earth. Not until there came a rattling of the chain at the cell door and a creaking of the rusty hinges did he lift his face. It was the jailer with a huge armful of straw. He saw Neil approach him after he had thrown it down. Their low voices came to him in an indistinct murmur. After a little he caught the sound of the chinking gold pieces.

Neil came and sat down beside him as the heavy door closed upon them again.

" He took it," he whispered exultantly. " He will deliver it this morning. If possible he will bring us an answer. I kept out a hundred and told him that a reply would be worth that to him."

Nathaniel did not speak, and after a moment's silence Neil continued.

" The jury is assembling. We will know our fate very soon."

He rose to his feet, his words quivering with nervous excitement, and Nathaniel heard him kicking about in the straw. In another breath his voice hissed through the gloom in a sharp, startled command:

" Good God, Nat, come here! "

Something in the strange fierceness of Neil's words startled Nathaniel, like the thrilling twinges of an electric shock. He darted across the cell and found Marion's brother with his shoulder against the door.

"It's open!" he whispered. "The door — is — open!"

The hinges creaked under his weight. A current of air struck them in the face. Another instant and they stood in the corridor, listening, crushing back the breath in their lungs, not daring to speak. Only the drip of water came to their ears. Gently Neil drew his companion back into the cell.

"There's a chance — one chance in ten thousand!" he whispered. "At the end of this corridor there is a door — the jailer's door. If that's not locked, we can make a run for it! I'd rather die fighting — than here!"

He slipped out again, pressing Nathaniel back.

"Wait for me!"

Nathaniel heard him stealing slowly through the blackness. A minute later he returned.

"Locked!" he exclaimed.

In the opposite direction a ray of light caught Nathaniel's eye.

"Where does that light come from?" he asked.

"Through a hole about as big as your two hands. It was made for a stove pipe. If we were up there we could see into the jury room."

They moved quietly down the corridor until they stood under the aperture, which was four or five feet above their heads. Through it they could hear the sound of voices but could not distinguish the words that were being spoken.

"The jury," explained Neil. "They're in a devil of a hurry! I wonder why?"

Nathaniel could feel his companion shrug himself in the darkness.

"Lord — for my revolver!" he whispered excitedly. "One shot through that hole would be worth a thousand notes to the girls!" He caught Marion's brother by the arm as a voice louder than the others came to them.

" Strang! "

" Yes — the — king! " affirmed Neil laying an expostulating hand on him. " Hush! "

" I would like to see —"

Even in these last hours of failure and defeat the fire of adventure flamed up in Nathaniel's blood. He felt his nerves leaping again to action, his arms grew tense with new ambition — almost he forgot that death had him cornered and was already preparing to strike him down. Another thought replaced all fear of this. A few feet beyond that log wall were gathered the men whose bloodthirsty deeds had written for them one of the reddest pages in history — men who had burned their souls out in the destruction of human lives, whose passions and loves and hatreds carried with them life and death; men who had bathed themselves in blood and lived in blood until the people of the mainland called them " the leeches."

247

" The Mormon jury! " Nathaniel spoke the words scarcely above his breath.

" I'd like to take a look through that hole, Neil," he added.

" Easy enough — if you keep quiet. Here! " He doubled himself against the wall. " Climb up on my shoulders."

No sooner had Nathaniel's face come to a level with the hole than a soft cry of astonishment escaped him. Neil whispered hoarsely but he did not reply. He was looking into a room twice as large as the dungeon cell and lighted by narrow windows whose lower panes were on a level with the ground outside. At the farther end of the room, in full view, was a platform raised several feet from the main floor. On this platform were seated ten men, immovable as statues, every face gazing straight ahead. Directly in front of them, on the lower floor, stood the Mormon king, and at his side, partly held in the embrace of one of his arms was Winnsome!

Strang's voice came to him in a low, solemn monotone, its rumbling depth drowning the words he was speaking, and as Nathaniel saw him lift his arm from about the girl's shoulders and place his great hand upon her head he dug his own fingers fiercely into the rotting logs and an imprecation burned in his breath. He did not need to hear what the king was saying. It was a pantomime in which every gesture was understandable. But even Neil, huddled against the wall, heard the last words of the prophet as they thundered forth in sudden passion.

" Winnsome Croche demands the death of her father's murderer ! "

Nathaniel felt his companion's shoulders sinking under his weight and he leaped quickly to the floor.

" Winnsome is there ! " he panted desperately. " Do you want to see her? "

Neil hesitated.

" No. Your boots gouge my shoulder. Take them off."

The scene had changed when Nathaniel took his position again. The jury had left its platform and was filing through a small door. Winnsome and the king were along.

The girl had turned from him. She was deathly pale and yet she was wondrously beautiful, so beautiful that Nathaniel's breath came in quick dread as the king approached her. He could see the triumph in his eyes, a terrible eagerness in his face. He seized Winnsome's hand and spoke to her in a soft, low voice, so low that it came to Nathaniel only in a murmur. Then, in a moment, he began stroking the shimmering glory of her hair, caressing the silken curls between his fingers until the blood seemed as if it must burst, like hot sweat from Nathaniel's face. Suddenly Winnsome drew back from him, the pallor gone from her face, her eyes blazing like angry stars. She had retreated but a step when the prophet sprang to her and caught her in his arms, straining her to him until the scream on her lips was choked to a gasping cry. In answer to that cry a yell of rage hurled itself from Nathaniel's throat.

"Stop, you hell-hound!" he cried threateningly. "Stop!"

He shrieked the words again and again, maddened beyond control, and the Mormon king, whose self-possession was more that of devil than man, still held the struggling girl in his arms as he turned his head toward the voice and saw Nathaniel's long arm and knotted fist threatening him through the hole in the wall. Then Neil's name in a piercing scream resounded through the dungeon corridor and in response to it the man under Nathaniel straightened himself so quickly that his companion fell back to the floor.

"Great God! what is the matter, Nat? Quick! let me up!"

Nathaniel staggered to his feet, the breath half gone out of his body, and in another instant Neil was at the opening. The great room into which he looked was empty.

"What was it?" he cried, leaping down. "What were they doing with Winnsome?"

"It was the king," said Nathaniel, struggling to master himself. "The king put his arms around Winnsome and — she struck him!"

"That was all?"

"He kissed her as she fought — and I yelled."

"She struck him!" Neil cried. "God bless little Winnsome, Nat! and — God bless her!"

Neil's breath came fast as he caught the other's hand.

"I'd give my life if I could help you — and Marion!"

"We'll give them together," said Nathaniel coolly, turning down the corridor. "Here's our chance. They'll come through that door to relock us in our cell. Shall we die fighting?"

He was groping about in the mud of the floor for some object.

"If we had a couple of stones —"

"It would be madness — worse than madness!" interposed Neil, steadying himself. "There will be a dozen rifles at that door when they open it. We must return to the cell. It is worth dying a harder death to hear from Marion and Winnsome. And we will hear from them before night!"

They retreated into the dungeon. A few minutes later the door opened cautiously at the head of the corridor. A light blazed through the blackness and after an interval of silence the jailer made his appearance in front of the cell, a pistol in his hand.

"Don't be afraid, Jeekum," said Neil reassuringly. "You forgot the door and we've been having a little fun with the jury. That's all!"

The nervous whiteness left Jeekum's face at this cheerful report and he was about to close the door when Nathaniel exhibited a handful of gold pieces in the candle-light and frantically beckoned the man to come in. The jailer's eyes glittered understandingly and with a backward glance down the lighted corridor he thrust his head and shoulders inside.

"Five hundred dollars for that note!" he whispered. "Five hundred beside the four you've got!"

"Jeekum's a fool!" said Neil, as the door closed on them. "I feel sorry for him."

"Why?"

"Because he is accepting the money. Don't you suppose that you have been searched? Of course you have — probably before I came, while you were half dead on the floor. Somebody knows that you have the gold."

"Why hasn't it been taken?"

For a full minute Neil made no answer. And his answer, when it did come, first of all was a laugh.

"By George, that's good!" he cried exultingly. "Of course you were searched — and by Jeekum! He knows, but he hasn't made a report of it to Strang because he believes that in some way he will get hold of the money. He is taking a big risk — but he's winning! I wonder what his first scheme was?"

"Thought I'd bury it, perhaps," vouchsafed Nathaniel, throwing himself upon the straw. "There's room for two here, Neil."

A long silence fell between them. The action during the last few minutes had been too great an effort for Nathaniel and his wound troubled him again. As the pain and his terrible thoughts of Marion's fate returned to him he regretted that they had not ended it all in one last fight at the door. There, at least, they might have died like men instead of waiting to be shot down like dogs, their hands bound behind them, their breasts naked to the Mormon rifles. He did not fear death. In more than one game he had played against its hand, more often for love of the sport than not, but there was a horror in being penned up and tortured by it. He had come to look upon it as a fair enemy, filled of course with subterfuge and treachery, which were the laws of the game; but he had

255

never dreamed of it as anything but merciful in its quickness. It was as if his adversary had broken an inviolable pact with him and he sweated and tossed on his bed of straw while Neil sat cool and silent on the bench against the dungeon wall. Sheer exhaustion brought him relief, and after a time he fell asleep.

He was awakened by Neil. The white face of Marion's brother was over him when he opened his eyes and he was shaking him roughly by the shoulder.

" Wake up, Nat! " he cried. " For Heaven's sake — wake up! "

He drew back as Nathaniel sleepily roused himself.

" I couldn't help it, Nat," he apologized, laughing nervously. " You've lain there like a dead man for hours. My head is splitting with this damned silence. Come — smoke up! I got some tobacco from our jailer and he loaned me his pipe."

Nathaniel jumped to his feet. A fresh candle

was burning on the table and in its light he saw that a startling change had come into Neil's face during the hours he had slept. It looked to him thinner and whiter, its lines had deepened, and the young man's eyes were filled with gloomy dejection.

" Why didn't you awaken me sooner? " he exclaimed. " I deserve a good drubbing for leaving you alone here! " He saw fresh food on the table. " It's late —" he began.

" That is our dinner and supper," interrupted Neil. He held his watch close to the candle. " Half past eight! "

" And no word — from —"

" No."

The two men looked deeply into each other's eyes.

" Jeekum delivered my note to her at noon when he was relieved," said Neil. " He did not carry it personally but swears that he saw her receive it. He sent her word that he would call at a certain place for a reply when he was relieved again at five. There was no reply for him — not a word from Winnsome."

Their silence was painful. It was Nathaniel who spoke first, hesitatingly, as though afraid to say what was passing in his mind.

"I killed Winnsome's father, Neil," he said, "and Winnsome has demanded my death. I know that I am condemned to die. But you —" His eyes flashed sudden fire. "How do you know that my fate is to be yours? I begin to see the truth. Winnsome has not answered your note because she knows that you are to live and that she will see you soon. Between Winnsome and — Marion you will be saved!"

Neil had taken a piece of meat and was eating it as though he had not heard his companion's words.

"Help yourself, Nat. It's our last opportunity."

"You don't believe —"

"No. Lord, man, do you suppose that Strang is going to let me live to kill him?"

Somebody was fumbling with the chain at the dungeon door.

The two men stared as it opened slowly and Jeekum appeared. The jailer was highly excited.

" I've got word — but no note! " he whispered hoarsely. " Quick! Is it worth —"

" Yes! Yes! "

Nathaniel dug the gold pieces out of his pockets and dropped them into the jailer's outstretched hand.

" I've had my boy watching Winnsome Croche's house," continued the sheriff, white with the knowledge of the risk he was taking. " An hour ago Winnsome came out of the house and went into the woods. My boy followed. She ran to the lake, got into a skiff, and rowed straight out to sea. She is following your instructions! "

In his excitement he betrayed himself. He had read the note.

There came a sound up the corridor, the opening of a door, the echo of voices, and Jeekum leaped back. Nathaniel's foot held the cell door from closing.

"Where is Marion?" he cried softly, his heart standing still with dread. "Great God — what about Marion?"

For an instant the sheriff's ghastly face was pressed against the opening.

"Marion has not been seen since morning. The king's officers are searching for her."

The door slammed, the chains clanked loudly, and above the sound of Jeekum's departure Neil's voice rose in a muffled cry of joy.

"They are gone! They are leaving the island!"

Nathaniel stood like one turned into stone. His heart grew cold within him. When he spoke his words were passionless echoes of what had been.

"You are sure that Marion would kill herself as soon as she became the wife of Strang?" he asked.

"Yes — before his vile hands touched more than the dress she wore!" shouted Neil.

"Then Marion is dead," replied Nathaniel, as coldly as though he were talking to the walls about him. "For last night Marion was forced into the harem of the king."

As he revealed the secret whose torture he meant to keep imprisoned in his own breast he dropped upon the pallet of straw and buried his face between his arms, cursing himself that he had weakened in these last hours of their comradeship.

He dared not look to see the effect of his words on Neil. His companion uttered no sound. Instead there was a silence that was terrifying.

At the end of it Neil spoke in a voice so strangely calm that Nathaniel sat up and stared at him through the gloom.

"I believe they are coming after us, Nat. Listen!"

The tread of many feet came to them faintly from beyond the corridor wall.

Nathaniel had risen. They drew close together, and their hands clasped.

" Whatever it may be," whispered Neil, " may God have mercy on our souls! "

" Amen! " breathed Captain Plum.

CHAPTER XI

HANDS were fumbling with the chain at the dungeon door.

It opened and Jeekum's ashen face shone in the candle-light. For a moment his frightened eyes rested on the two men still standing in their last embrace of friendship. A word of betrayal from them and he knew that his own doom was sealed.

He came in, followed by four men. One of them was MacDougall, the king's whipper. In the corridor were other faces, like ghostly shadows in the darkness. Only MacDougall's face was uncovered. The others were hidden behind white masks. The men uttered no sound but ranged themselves like specters in front of the door, their cocked rifles swung into the crooks

263

of their arms. There was a triumphant leer on MacDougall's lips as he and the jailer approached. As the whipper bound Neil's hands behind his back he hissed in his ear.

" This will be a better job than the whipping, damn you! "

Neil laughed.

" Hear that, Nat? " he asked, loud enough for all in the cell to hear. " MacDougall says this will be a better job than the whipping. He remembers how I thrashed him once when he said something to Marion one day."

Neil was as cool as though acting his part in a play. His face was flushed, his eyes gleamed fearlessly defiant. And Nathaniel, looking upon the courage of this man, from under whose feet had been swept all hope of life, felt a twinge of shame at his own nervousness. MacDougall grew black with passion at the taunting reminder of his humiliation and tightened the thongs about Neil's wrists until they cut into the flesh.

THE STRAIGHT DEATH

" That's enough, you coward!" exclaimed Nathaniel, as he saw the blood start. " Here — take this!"

Like lightning he struck out and his fist fell with crushing force against the side of the man's head. MacDougall toppled back with a hollow groan, blood spurting from his mouth and nose. Nathaniel turned coolly to the four rifles leveled at his breast.

" A pretty puppet to do the king's commands!" he cried. " If there's a man among you let him finish the work!"

Jeekum had fallen upon his knees beside the whipper.

" Great God!" he shrieked. " You've killed him! You've stove in the side of his head!"

There was a sudden commotion in the corridor. A terrible voice boomed forth in a roar.

" Let me in!"

Strang stood in the door. He gave a single glance at the man gasping and bleeding in the mud. Then he looked at Nathaniel. The eyes of the two men met unflinching. There was no hatred now in the prophet's face.

" Captain Plum, I would give a tenth of my kingdom for a brother like you! " he said calmly. " Here — I will finish the work." He went boldly to the task, and as he tied Nathaniel's arms behind him he added, " The vicissitudes of war, Captain Plum. You are a man — and can appreciate what they sometimes mean! "

A few minutes later, gagged and bound, the prisoners fell behind two of the armed guards and at a command from the king, given in a low tone to Jeekum, marched through the corridor and up the short flight of steps that led out of the jail. To Nathaniel's astonishment there was no light to guide them. Candles and lights had been extinguished. What words he heard were spoken in whispers. In the deep shadow of the prison wall a third guard joined the two ahead and like automatons they strode through the gloom with slow, measured step, their rifles held with soldierly precision. Nathaniel glanced over his shoulder and saw three other white masked faces a dozen feet away. The king had remained behind.

He shuddered and looked at Neil. His companion's appearance was almost startling. He seemed half a head taller than himself, yet he knew that he was shorter by an inch or two; his shoulders were thrown back, his chin held high, he kept step with the guards ahead. He was marching to his death as coolly as though on parade.

Nathaniel's heart beat excitedly as they came to where the scrub of the forest met the plain. They were taking the path that led to Marion's! Again he looked at Neil. There was no change in the fearless attitude of Marion's brother, no lowering of his head, no faltering in his step. They passed the graves and entered the opening in the forest where lay Marion's home, and as once more the sweet odor of lilac came to him, awakening within his soul all those things that he had tried to stifle that he might meet death

like a man, he felt himself weakening, until only
the cloth about his mouth restrained the moaning cry that forced itself to his lips. If he had
possessed a life to give he would have sacrificed
it gladly then for a word with the Mormon king,
a last prayer that death might be meted to him
here, where eternity would come to him with his
glazing eyes fixed to the end upon the home
of his beloved, and where the sweetness of the
flower that had become a part of Marion herself might soothe the pain of his final moment on
earth.

His heart leaped with hope as a sharp voice
from the rear commanded a halt. It was Jeekum. He came up out of the darkness from
behind the rear guard, his face still unmasked,
and for a few moments was in whispered con-
sultation with the guards ahead. Had Strang,
in the virulence of that hatred which he concealed so well, conceived of this spot to give
added torment to death? It was the poetry of
vengeance! For the first time Neil turned to-

ward his companion. Each read what the other
had guessed. Neil, who was nearest to the
whispering four, turned suddenly toward them
and listened. When he looked at Nathaniel
again it was with a slow negative shake of his
head.

Jeekum returned quickly and placed himself
between them, seizing each by an arm, and the
forward guards, pivoting to the left, set off at
their steady pace across the clearing. As they
entered the denser gloom of the forest on the
farther side Nathaniel felt the jailer's fingers
tighten about his arm, then relax — and tighten
again. A gentle pressure held him back and the
guards in front gained half a dozen feet. In
a low voice Jeekum called for those behind to
fall a few paces to the rear.

Then came again the mysterious working of
the man's fingers on Nathaniel's arm.

Was Jeekum signaling to him?

He could see Neil's white face still turned
stoically to the front. Evidently nothing had

occurred to arouse his suspicions. If the maneuvering of Jeekum's fingers meant anything it was intended for him alone. Action had been the manna of his life. The possibility of new adventure, even in the face of death, thrilled him. He waited, breathless — and the strange pressure came again, so hard that it hurt his flesh.

There was no longer a doubt in his mind. The king's sheriff wanted to speak to him.

And he was afraid of the eyes and ears behind.

The fingers were cautioning him to be ready — when the opportunity came.

The path widened and through the thin tree-tops above their heads the starlight filtered down upon them. The leading guards were twenty feet away. How far behind were the others?

A moment more and they plunged into deep night again. The figures ahead were mere shadows. Again the fingers dug into Nathaniel's arm, and pressing close to the sheriff he bent down his head.

A low, quick whisper fell in his ear.

"Don't give up hope! Marion — Winnsome —"

The sheriff jerked himself erect without finishing. Hurried footsteps had come close to their heels. The rear guards were so near that they could have touched them with their guns. Had some spot of lesser gloom ahead betrayed the prisoner's bowed head and Jeekum's white face turned to it? There was a steady pressure on Nathaniel's arm now, a warning, frightened pressure, and the hand that made it trembled. Jeekum feared the worst — but his fear was not greater than the chill of disappointment that came to smother the excited beating of Nathaniel's heart. What had the jailer meant to say? What did he know about Marion and Winnsome, and why had he given birth to new hope in the same breath that he mentioned their names?

His words carried at least one conviction. Marion was alive despite her brother's somber prophesies. If she had killed herself the sheriff would not have coupled her name with Winnsome's in the way he had.

Nathaniel's nerves were breaking with suspense. He stifled his breath to listen, to catch the faintest whisper that might come to him from the white faced man at his side. Each passing moment of silence added to his desperation. He squeezed the sheriff's hand with his arm, but there was no responding signal; in a patch of thick gloom that almost concealed the figures ahead he pressed near to him and lowered his head again — and Jeekum pushed him back fiercely, with a low curse.

They emerged from the forest and the clear starlight shone down upon them. A little distance off lay the lake in shimmering stillness. Nathaniel looked boldly at the sheriff now, and as his glance passed beyond him he was amazed at the change that had come over Neil. The young man's head was bowed heavily upon his breast, his shoulders were hunched forward, and he walked with a listless, uneven step. Was it possible that his magnificent courage had at last given way?

A hundred steps farther they came to the beach and Nathaniel saw a boat at the water's edge with a single figure guarding it. Straight to this Jeekum led his prisoners. For the first time he spoke to them aloud.

"One in front, the other in back," he said.

For an instant Nathaniel found himself close beside Neil and he prodded him sharply with his knee. His companion did not lift his head. He made no sign, gave no last flashing comradeship with his eyes, but climbed into the bow of the boat and sat down with his chin still on his chest, like a man lost in stupor.

Nathaniel followed him, scarcely believing his eyes, and sat himself in the stern, leaning comfortably against the knees of the man who took the tiller. He felt a curious thrill pass through him when he discovered a moment later that this man was Jeekum. Two men seized the oars amidships. A fourth, with his rifle across his knees sat facing Neil.

For the first time Nathaniel found himself wondering what this voyage meant. Were they to be rowed far down the shore to some secret fastness where no other ears would hear the sound of the avenging rifles, and where, a few inches under the forest mold, their bodies would never be discovered? Each stroke of the oars added to the remoteness of this possibility. The boat was heading straight out to sea. Perhaps they were to meet a less terrible death by drowning, an end which, though altogether unpleasant, held something comforting in it for Captain Plum. Two hours passed without pause in the steady labor of the men at the oars. In those hours not a word was spoken. The two men amidships held no communication. The guard in the bow moved a little now and then only to relieve his cramped limbs. Neil was absolutely motionless, as though he had ceased to breathe. Jeekum uttered not a whisper.

It was his whisper that Nathaniel waited for, the signaling clutch of his fingers, the sound of his breath close to his ears. Again and again he pressed himself against the sheriff's knees. He knew that he was understood, and yet there came no answer. At last he looked up, and Jeekum's face was far above him, staring straight and unseeing into the darkness ahead. His last spark of hope went out.

After a time a dark rim loomed slowly up out of the sea. It was land, half a mile or so away. Nathaniel sat up with fresh interest, and as they drew nearer Jeekum rose to his feet and gazed long and steadily in both directions along the coast. When he returned to his seat the boat's course was changed. A few minutes later the bow grated upon sand. Still voiceless as specters the guards leaped ashore and Neil roused himself to follow them, climbing over the gunwale like a sick man. Nathaniel was close at his heels. With a growing sense of horror he saw two ghostly stakes thrusting themselves out of the beach a dozen paces away. He looked beyond them. As far as he could see there was sand — nothing but sand, as white as paper, scintillating in a billion flashing needle-points in the starlight. Instinctively he guessed what the stakes were for, and walked toward them with the blood turning cold in his veins. Neil was before him and stopped at the first stake, making no effort to lift his eyes as Nathaniel strode past him. At the second, a dozen feet beyond, Nathaniel's two guards halted, and placed him with his back to the post. Two minutes later, bound hand and foot to the stake, he shifted his head so that he could look at his companion.

Neil was similarly fastened, with his face turned partly toward him. There was no change in his attitude. His head hung weakly upon his chest, as if he had fainted.

What did it mean?

Suddenly every nerve in Nathaniel's body leaped into excited action.

The guards were entering their boat! The last man was shoving it off — they were rowing away! His throbbing muscles seemed ready to burst their bonds. The boat became indistinct in the starry gloom — a mere shadow — and faded in the distance. The sound of oars became fainter and fainter. Then, after a little, there was wafted back to him from far out in the lake a man's voice — the wild snatch of a song. The Mormons were gone! They were not to be shot! They were not —

A voice spoke to him, startling him so that he would have cried out if it had not been for the cloth that gagged him. It was Neil, speaking coolly, laughingly.

" How are you, Nat? "

Nathaniel's staring eyes revealed his astonishment. He could see Neil laughing at him as though it was an unusually humorous joke in which they were playing a part.

"Lord, but this is a funny mess!" he chuckled. "Here am I, able and willing to talk — and there you are, as dumb as a mummy, and looking for all the world as if you'd seen a ghost! What's the matter? Aren't you glad we're not going to be shot?"

Nathaniel nodded.

The other's voice became suddenly sober.

"This is worse than the other, Nat. It's what we call the 'Straight Death.' Unless something turns up between now and to-morrow morning, or a little later, we'll be as dead as though they had filled us with bullets. Our only hope rests in the fact that I can use my lungs. That's why I didn't let them know when my gag became loose. I had the devil's own time keeping it from falling with my chin; pretty near broke my neck doing it. A little later, when we're sure Jeekum and his men are out of hearing, I'll begin calling for help. Perhaps some fisherman or hunter —"

He stopped, and a chill ran up Nathaniel's

back as he listened to a weird howl that came from far behind them. It was a blood-curdling sound and his face turned a more ghastly pallor as he gazed inquiringly at Neil. His companion saw the terrible question in his face.

" Wolves," he said. " They're away back in the forest. They won't come down to us." For a moment he was silent, his eyes turned to the sea. Then he added, " Do you notice anything queer about the way you're bound to that stake, Nat? "

There was a thrilling emphasis in Nathaniel's answer. He nodded his head affirmatively, again and again.

" Your hands are tied to the post very loosely, with a slack of say six inches," continued Neil with an appalling precision. " There is a rawhide thong about your neck, wet, and so tight that it chafes your skin when you move your head. But the very uncomfortable thing just at this moment is the way your feet are fastened. Isn't that so? Your legs are drawn back, so

that you are half resting on your toes, and I'm
pretty sure your knees are aching right now.
Eh? Well, it won't be very long before your
legs will give way under you and the slack about
your wrists will keep you from helping yourself. Do you know what will happen then? "

He paused and Nathaniel stared at him,
partly understanding, yet giving no sign.

" You will hang upon the thong about your
neck until you choke to death," finished Neil.
" That's the ' Straight Death.' If the end
doesn't come by morning the sun will finish the
job. It will dry out the wet rawhide until it
grips your throat like a hand. Poetically we
call it the hand of Strang. Pleasant, isn't it? "

The grim definiteness with which he described
the manner of their end added to those sensations which had already become acutely discom-
forting to Nathaniel. Had he possessed the use
of his voice when the Mormons were leaving he
would have called upon them to return and
lengthen the thongs about his ankles by an inch

or two. Now, with almost brutal frankness, Neil had explained to him the meaning of his strange posture. His knees began to ache. An occasional sharp pain shot up from them to his hips, and the thong about his neck, which at first he had used as a support for his chin, began to irritate him. At times he found himself resting upon it so heavily that it shortened his breath, and he was compelled to straighten himself, putting his whole weight on his twisted feet. It seemed an hour before Neil broke the terrible silence again. Perhaps it was ten minutes.

"I'm going to begin," he said. "Listen. If you hear an answer nod your head."

He drew a deep breath, turned his face as far as he could toward the shore, and shouted.

"Help — help — help!"

Again and again the thrilling words burst from his throat, and as their echoes floated back to them from the forest, like a thousand mocking voices, Nathaniel grew hot with the sweat of horror. If he could only have added his own voice to those cries, shrieked out the words with Neil — joined even unavailingly in this last fight for life, it would not have been so bad. But he was helpless. He watched the desperation grow in his companion's face as there came no response save the taunting echoes; even in the light of the stars he saw that face darken with its effort, the eyes fill with a mad light, and the throat strain against its choking thong. Gradually Neil's voice became weaker. When he stopped to rest and listen his panting breath came to Nathaniel like the hissing of steam. Soon the echoes failed to come back from the forest, and Nathaniel fought like a crazed man to free himself, jerking at the thongs that held him until his wrists were bleeding and the rawhide about his neck choked him.

"No use!" he heard Neil say. "Better take it easy for a while, Nat!"

Marion's brother had turned toward him, his head thrown back against the stake, his face lifted to the sky. Nathaniel raised his own head, and found that he could breath easier. For a long time his companion did not break the silence. Mentally he began counting off the seconds. It was past midnight — probably one o'clock. Dawn came at half past two, the sun rose an hour later. Three hours to live! Nathaniel lowered his head, and the rawhide tightened perceptibly at the movement. Neil was watching him. His face shone as white as the starlit sand. His mouth was partly open.

" I'm devilish sorry — for you — Nat —" he said.

His words came with painful slowness. There was a grating huskiness in his voice.

" This damned rawhide — is pinching — my Adam's apple —"

He smiled. His white teeth gleamed, his eyes laughed, and with a heart bursting with grief Nathaniel looked away from him. He had seen courage, but never like this, and deep down in his soul he prayed — prayed that death might come to him first, so that he might not have to look upon the agonies of this other, whose end would be ghastly in its fearless resignation. His own suffering had become excruciating. Sharp pains darted like red-hot needles through his limbs, his back tortured him, and his head ached as though a knife had cloven the base of his skull. Still — he could breathe. By pressing his head against the post it was not difficult for him to fill his lungs with air. But the strength of his limbs was leaving him. He no longer felt any sensation in his cramped feet. His knees were numb. He measured the paralysis of death creeping up his legs inch by inch, driving the sharp pains before it, until suddenly his weight tottered under him and he hung heavily upon the thong about his throat. For a full half minute he ceased to breathe, and a feeling of ineffable relief swept over him, for during those few seconds his body was at rest. He found that by a backward contortion he could bring himself erect again, and that for a few minutes after each respite it was not so difficult for him to stand.

After a third effort he turned again toward Neil. A groan of horror rose to his imprisoned lips. His companion's face was full upon him, ghastly white; his eyes were wide and staring, like balls of shimmering glass in the starlight, and his throat was straining at the fatal rawhide! Nathaniel heard no sound, saw no stir of life in the inanimate figure.

A moaning, wordless cry broke through the cloth that gagged him.

At the sound of that cry, faint, terrifying, with all the horror that might fill a human soul in its inarticulate note, a shudder of life passed into Neil's body. Weakly he flung himself back, stood poised for an instant against the stake, then fell again upon the deadly thong. Twice — three times he made the effort, and failed. And to Nathaniel, staring wild eyed and silent now, the spectacle was one that seemed to blast the very soul within him and send his blood in rushing torrents of fire to his sickened brain. Neil was dying! A fourth time he struggled back. A fifth — and he held his ground. Even in that passing instant something like a flash of his buoyant smile flickered in his face and there came to Nathaniel's ears like a throttled whisper — his name.

" Nat —"

And no more.

The head fell forward again. And Nathaniel, turning his face away, saw something come up out of the shimmering sea, like a shadow before his blistering eyes, and as his own limbs went out from under him and he felt the strangling death at his throat there came from that shadow a cry that seemed to snap his very heartstrings — a piercing cry and (even in his half consciousness he recognized it) a woman's cry! He flung himself back, and for a moment he saw Neil struggling, the last spark of life in him stirred by that same cry; and then across the white sand two figures flew madly toward them and even as the hot film in his eyes grew thicker he knew that one of them was Marion, and that the other was Winnsome Croche.

His heart seemed to stop beating. He strove to pull himself together, but his head fell forward. Faintly, as on a battlefield, voices came to him, and when with a superhuman effort he straightened himself for an instant he saw that Neil was no longer at the stake but was stretched on the sand, and of the two figures beside him one suddenly sprang to her feet and ran to him. And then Marion's terror-filled face was close to his own, and Marion's lips were moaning his name, and Marion's hands were slashing at the thongs that bound him. When with a great sigh of joy he crumpled down upon the earth he knew that he was slipping off into oblivion with Marion's arms about his neck, and with her lips pressing to his the sweet elixir of her love.

Darkness enshrouded him but a few moments, when a dash of cool water brought him back into light. He felt himself lowered upon the sand and after a breath or two he twisted himself on his elbow and saw that Neil's white face was held on Winnsome's breast and that Marion was running up from the shore with more water. For a space she knelt beside her brother, and then she hurried to him. Joy shone in her face. She fell upon her knees and drew his head in the hollow of her arm, crooning mad senseless words to him, and bathing his face with water, her eyes shining down upon him gloriously. Nathaniel reached up and touched her face, and she bowed her head until her hair smothered him in sweet gloom, and kissed him. He drew her lips to his own, and then she lowered him gently and stood up in the starlight, looking first at Neil and next down at him; and then she turned quickly back to the sea.

From down near the shore she called back some word, and with a shrill cry Winnsome followed her. Nathaniel struggled to his elbow, to his knees — staggered to his feet. He saw the boat drifting out into the night, and Winnsome standing alone at the water-edge, her sobbing cries of entreaty, of terror, following it unanswered. He tottered down toward her, gaining new strength at each step, but when he reached her the boat was no longer to be seen and Winnsome's face was whiter than the sands under her feet.

" She is gone — gone —" she moaned, stretching out her arms to him. " She is going — back to Strang!"

And then, from far out in the white glory of the night, there came back to him the voice of the girl he loved.

" Good-by — Good-by—"

CHAPTER XII

MARION FREED FROM BONDAGE

"Gone!" moaned Winnsome again. " She has gone — back — to — Strang!"

Neil was crawling to them like a wounded animal across the sand.

She started toward him but Nathaniel stopped her.

" She is the king's — wife —"

His throat was swollen so that he could hardly speak.

" No. They are to be married to-night. Oh, I thought she was going to stay!" She tore herself away from him to go to Neil, who had fallen upon his face exhausted, a dozen yards away.

In the wet sand, where the incoming waves

lapped his hands and feet, Nathaniel sank down, his eyes staring out into the shimmering distance where Marion had gone. His brain was in a daze, and he wondered if he had been stricken by some strange madness — if this all was but some passing phantasm that would soon leave him again to his misery and his despair. But the dash of the cold water against him cleared away his doubt. Marion had come to him. She had saved him from death. And now she was gone.

And she was not the king's wife!

He staggered to his feet again and plunged into the lake until the water reached to his waist, calling her name, entreating her in weak, half choked cries to come back to him. The water soaked through to his hot, numb body, restoring his reason and strength, and he buried his face in it and drank like one who had been near to dying of thirst. Then he returned to Neil. Winnsome was holding his head in her arms.

He dropped upon his knees beside them and

saw that life was returning full and strong in Neil's face.

"You will be able to walk in a few minutes," he said. "You and Winnsome must leave here. We are on the mainland and if you follow the shore northward you will come to the settlements. I am going back for Marion."

Neil made an effort to follow him as he rose to his feet.

"Nat — Nat — wait —"

Winnsome held him back, frightened, tightening her arms about him.

"You must go with Winnsome," urged Nathaniel, seizing the hand that Neil stretched up to him. "You must take her to the first settlement up the coast. I will come back to you with Marion."

He spoke confidently, as a man who sees his way open clearly before him, and yet as he turned, half running, to the low black shadow of the distant forest he knew that he was beginning a blind fight against fate. If he could find a hunter's cabin, a fisherman's shanty — a boat!

Barely had he disappeared when a voice called to him. It was Winnsome. The girl ran up to him holding something in her hand. It was a pistol. "You may need it!" she exclaimed. "We brought two!"

Nathaniel reached out hesitatingly, but not to take the weapon. Gently, as though his touch was about to fall upon some fragile flower, he drew the girl to him, took her beautiful face between his two strong hands and gazed steadily and silently for a moment into her eyes.

"God bless you, little Winnsome!" he whispered. "I hope that some day you will — forgive me."

The girl understood him.

"If I have anything to forgive — you are forgiven."

The pistol dropped upon the sand, her hands stole to his shoulders.

"I want you to take something to Marion for me," she whispered softly. "This!"

And she kissed him.

Her eyes shone upon him like a benediction.

"You have given me a new life, you have given me — Neil! My prayers are with you."

And kissing him again, she slipped away from under his hands before he could speak.

And Nathaniel, following her with his eyes until he could no longer see her, picked up the pistol and set off again toward the forest, the touch of her lips and the prayers of this girl whose father he had slain filling him with something that was more than strength, more than hope. Life had been given to him again, strong, fighting life, and with it and Winnsome's words there returned his old confidence, his old daring. There was everything for him to win now. His doubts and his fears had been swept away. Marion was not dead, she was not the king's wife — and it was not of another that he had accepted proof of her love for him, for he had

felt the pressure of her arms about his neck
and the warmth of her lips upon his face. He
had until night — and the dawn was just beginning to break. Ten or fifteen miles to the
north there were settlements, and between there
were scores of settlers' homes and fishermen's
shanties. Surely within an hour or two he
would find a boat.

He turned where the edge of the forest came
down to meet the white water-run of the sea, and
set off at a slow, steady trot into the north. If
he could reach a boat soon he might overtake
Marion in mid-lake. The thought thrilled him,
and urged him to greater speed. As the stars
faded away in the dawn he saw the dark barrier
of the forest drifting away, and later, when the
light broke more clearly, there stretched out
ahead of him mile upon mile of desert dunes.
As far as he could see there was no hope of life.
He slowed his steps now, for he would need to
preserve his strength. Yet he experienced no
fear, no loss of confidence. Each moment added

to his faith in himself. Before noon he would be on his way to the Mormon kingdom, by nightfall he would be upon its shores. After that —

He examined the pistol that Winnsome had given him. There were five shots in it and he smiled joyously as he saw that it had been loaded by an experienced hand. It would be easy enough for him to find Strang. He would not consider the woman — his wife. The king's wife! Like a flash there occurred to him the incident of the battle-field. Was it this woman — the woman who had begged him to spare the life of the prophet, who had knelt beside him, and whispered in his ear, and kissed him? Had that been her reward for the sacrifice she believed he had made for her in the castle chamber? The thought of this woman, whose beauty and love breathed the sweet purity of a flower and whose faith to her king and master was still unbroken even in her hour of repudiation fell upon him heavily. For there was no choice, no shadow of alternative. There was but one way for him to break the bondage of the girl he loved.

For hours he trod steadily through the sand. The sun rose above him, hot and blistering, and the dunes still stretched out ahead of him, like winnows and hills and mountains of glittering glass. Gradually the desert became narrower. Far ahead he could see where the forest came down to the shore and his heart grew lighter. Half an hour later he entered the margin of trees. Almost immediately he found signs of life. A tree had been felled and cut into wood. A short distance beyond he came suddenly upon a narrow path, beaten hard by the passing of feet, and leading toward the lake. He had meant to rest under the shade of these trees but now he forgot his fatigue. For a moment he hesitated. Far back in the forest he heard the barking of a dog — but he turned in the opposite direction. If there was a boat the path would take him to it. Through a break in the trees he caught the green sweep of marsh rice and his heart beat excitedly with hope. Where there was rice there were wild-fowl, and surely where there were wild-fowl, there would be a punt or a canoe! In his eagerness he ran, and where the path ended, the flags and rice beaten into the mud and water, he stopped with an exultant cry. At his feet was a canoe. It was wet, as though just drawn out of the water, and a freshly used paddle was lying across the bow. Pausing but to take a quick and cautious glance about him he shoved the frail craft into the lake and with a few quiet strokes buried himself in the rice grass. When he emerged from it he was half a mile from the shore.

For a long time he sat motionless, looking out over the shimmering sea. Far to the south and west he could make out the dim outline of Beaver Island, while over the trail he had come, mile upon mile, lay the glistening dunes. Somewhere between the white desert sand and that distant coast of the Mormon kingdom Marion was making her way back to bondage. Nathaniel had given up all hope of overtaking her now. Long before he could intercept her she would have reached the island. When he started again he paddled slowly, and laid out for himself the plan that he was to follow. There must be no mistake this time, no error in judgment, no rashness in his daring. He would lie in hiding until dusk, and then under cover of darkness he would hunt down Strang and kill him. After that he would fly to his canoe and escape. A little later, perhaps that very night if fate played the game well for him, he would return for Marion. And yet, as he went over and over his scheme, whipping himself into caution — into cool deliberation — there burned in his blood a fire that once or twice made him set his teeth hard, a fire that defied extinction, that smoldered only to await the breath that would fan it into a fierce blaze. It was the fire that had urged him into the rescue at the whipping-post, that had sent him single-handed to invade the king's castle, that had hurled him into the hopeless battle upon the shore. He swore at himself softly, laughingly, as he paddled steadily toward Beaver Island.

The sun mounted straight and hot over his head; he paddled more slowly, and rested more frequently, as it descended into the west, but it still lacked two hours of sinking behind the island forest when the white water-run of the shore came within his vision. He had meant to hold off the coast until the approach of evening but changed his mind and landed, concealing his canoe in a spot which he marked well, for he knew it would soon be useful to him again. Deep shadows were already gathering in the forest and through these Nathaniel made his way slowly in the direction of St. James. Between him and the town lay Marion's home and the path that led to Obadiah's. Once more the spirit of impatience, of action, stirred within him. Would Marion go first to her home? Involuntarily he changed his course so that it would bring him to the clearing. He assured himself that it would do no harm, that he still would take no chances.

He came out in the strip of dense forest between the clearing and St. James, worming his way cautiously through the underbrush until he could look out into the opening. A single glance and he drew back in astonishment. He looked again, and his face turned suddenly white, and an almost inaudible cry fell from his lips. There was no longer a cabin in the clearing! Where it had been there was gathered a crowd of men and boys. Above their heads he saw a thin film of smoke and he knew what had happened. Marion's home had burned! But what was the crowd doing? It hung close in about the smoldering ruins as if every person in it were striving to reach a common center. Surely a mere fire would not gather and hold a throng like this.

Nathaniel rose to his feet and thrust his head and shoulders from his hiding-place. He heard a loud shout near him and drew back quickly as a boy rushed madly across the opening toward the crowd, crying out at the top of his voice. He had come out of the path that led to St. James. No sooner had he reached the group about the burned cabin than there came a change that added to Nathaniel's bewilderment. He heard loud voices, the excited shouting of men and the shrill cries of boys, and the crowd suddenly began to move, thinning itself out until it was racing in a black stream toward the Mormon city. In his excitement Nathaniel hurried toward the path. From the concealment of a clump of bushes he watched the people as they rushed past him a dozen paces away. Behind all the others there came a figure that drew a sharp cry from him as he leaped from his hiding-place. It was Obadiah Price.

"Obadiah!" he called. "Obadiah Price!"

The old man turned. His face was livid. He was chattering to himself, and he chattered still as he ran up to Nathaniel. He betrayed no surprise at seeing him, and yet there was the insane grip of steel in the two hands that clutched fiercely at Nathaniel's.

"You have come in time, Nat!" he panted joyfully. "You have come in time! Hurry — hurry — hurry —"

He ran back into the clearing, with Nathaniel close at his side, and pointed to the smoking ruins of the cabin among the lilacs.

"They were killed last night!" he cried shrilly. "Somebody murdered them — and burned them with the house! They are dead — dead!"

"Who?" shouted Nathaniel.

Obadiah had stopped and was rubbing and twisting his hands in his old, mad way.

"The old folks. Ho, ho, the old folks, of course! They are dead — dead — dead —"

He fairly shrieked the words. Then, for a moment, he stood tightly clutching his thin hands over his chest in a powerful effort to control himself.

"They are dead!" he repeated.

He spoke more calmly, and yet there was something so terrible in his eyes, something so harshly vibrant of elation in the quivering passion of his voice that Nathaniel felt himself filled with a strange horror. He caught him by the arm, shaking him as he would have shaken a child.

"Where is Marion?" he asked. "Tell me, Obadiah — where is Marion?"

The councilor seemed not to have heard him. A singular change came into his face and his eyes traveled beyond Nathaniel. Following his glance the young man saw that three men had appeared from the scorched shrubbery about the burned house and were hurrying toward them. Without shifting his eyes Obadiah spoke to him quickly.

"Those are king's sheriffs, Nat," he said. "They know me. In a moment they will recognize you. The United States warship *Michigan* has just arrived in the harbor to arrest Strang. If you can reach the cabin and hold it for an hour you will be saved. Quick — you must run —"

"Where is Marion?"

" At the cabin! She is at —"

Nathaniel waited to hear no more, but sped toward the breach in the forest that marked the beginning of the path to Obadiah's. The shouts of the king's men came to him unheeded. At the edge of the woods he glanced back and saw that they had overtaken the councilor. As he ran he drew his pistol and in his wild joy he flung back a shout of defiance to the men who were pursuing him. Marion was at the cabin — and a government ship had come to put an end to the reign of the Mormon king! He shouted Marion's name as he came in sight of the cabin; he cried it aloud as he bounded up the low steps.

" Marion — Marion —"

In front of the door that led to the tiny chamber in which he had taken Obadiah's gold he saw a figure. For a moment he was blinded by his sudden dash from the light of day into the gloom of the cabin, and he saw only that a figure was standing there, as still as death. His pistol dropped to the floor. He stretched out his arms, and his voice sobbed in its entreaty as he whispered the girl's name. In response to that whisper came a low, glad cry, and Marion lay trembling on his breast.

" I have come back for you! " he breathed.

He felt her heart beating against him. He pressed her closer, and her arms slipped about his neck.

" I have come back for you! "

He was almost crying, like a boy, in his happiness.

" I love you, I love you — "

He felt the warm touch of her lips.

" You will go with me? "

" If you want me," she whispered. " If you want me — after you know — what I am —"

She shuddered against his breast, and he raised her face between his two hands and kissed her until she drew away from him, crying softly.

Marion

" You must wait — you must wait! "

He saw now in her face an agony that appalled him. He would have gone to her again, but there came loud voices from the forest, and recovering his pistol he sprang to the door. Half a hundred paces away were Obadiah and the king's sheriffs. They had stopped and the councilor was expostulating excitedly with the men, evidently trying to keep them from the cabin. Suddenly one of the three broke past him and ran swiftly toward the open door, and with a shriek of warning to Nathaniel the old councilor drew a pistol and fired point blank in the sheriff's back. In another instant the two men behind had fired and Obadiah fell forward upon his face.

With a yell of rage Nathaniel leaped from the door. He heard Marion cry out his name, but his fighting blood was stirred and he did not stop. Obadiah had given up his life for him, for Marion, and he was mad with a desire to wreak vengeance upon the murderers. The first

man lay where he had fallen, with Obadiah's
bullet through his back. The other two fired
again as Nathaniel rushed down upon them.
He heard the zip of one of the balls, which came
so close that it stung his cheek.

" Take that! " he cried.

He fired, still running — once, twice, three
times and one of the two men crumpled down as
though a powerful blow had broken his legs
under him.

The other turned into the path and ran.
Nathaniel caught a glimpse of a frightened,
boyish face, and something of mercy prompted
him to hold the shot he was about to send
through his lungs.

" Stop! " he shouted. " Stop! "

He aimed at the fugitive's legs and fired.

" Stop! "

The boyish sheriff was lengthening the distance between them and Nathaniel halted to
make sure of his last ball. He was about to
shoot when there came a sharp command from

down the path and a file of men burst into view, running at double-quick. He saw the flash of a saber, the gleam of brass buttons, the blue glare of the setting sun on leveled carbines, and he stopped, shoulder to shoulder with the man he had been pursuing. For a moment he stared as the man with the naked saber approached. Then he sprang toward him with a joyful cry of recognition.

" My God, Sherly — Sherly —"

He stood with his arms stretched out, his naked chest heaving.

" Sherly — Lieutenant Sherly — don't you know me? "

The lieutenant had dropped the point of his saber. He advanced a step, his face filled with astonishment.

" Plum ! " he cried incredulously. " Is it you? "

For the moment Nathaniel could only wring the other's hand. He tried to speak but his breath choked him.

" I told you in Chicago that I was going to blow up this damned island — if you wouldn't do it for me —" he gasped at last. " I've had — a hell of a time —"

" You look it!" laughed the lieutenant. " We got our orders the second day after you left to ' Arrest Strang, and break up the Mormon kingdom!' We've got Strang aboard the *Michigan*. But he's dead."

" Dead! "

" He was shot in the back by one of his own men as we were bringing him up the gang-way. The fellow who killed him has given himself up, and says that he did it because Strang had him publicly whipped day before yesterday. I'm up here hunting for a man named Obadiah Price. Do you know —"

Nathaniel interrupted him excitedly.

" What do you want with Obadiah Price? "

" The president of the United States wants him. That's all I know. Where is he? "

" Back there — dead or very badly wounded!

310

We've just had a fight with the king's men —"

The lieutenant broke in with a sharp command to his men.

" Quick, lead us to him. Captain Plum! If he's not dead —"

He started off at a half run beside Nathaniel.

" Lord, it's a pretty mess if he is!" he added breathlessly. Without pausing he called back over his shoulder, " Regan, fall out and return to the ship. Tell the captain that Obadiah Price is badly wounded and that we want the surgeon on the run!"

A turn in the path brought them to the opening where the fight had occurred. Marion was on her knees beside the old councilor.

Nathaniel hurried ahead of the lieutenant and his men. The girl glanced up at him and his heart filled with dread at the terror in her eyes.

" Is he dead? "

" No — but —" Her voice trembled with tears.

Nathaniel did not let her finish. Gently he

311

raised her to her feet as the lieutenant came up.

"You must go to the cabin, sweetheart," he whispered.

Even in this moment of excitement and death his great love drove all else from his eyes, and the blood surged into Marion's pale cheeks as she tremblingly gave him her hand. He led her to the door, and held her for a moment in his arms.

"Strang is dead," he said softly. In a few words he told her what had happened and turned back to the door, leaving her speechless.

"If he is dying — you will tell me —" she called after him.

"Yes, yes, I will tell you."

He ran back into the opening.

The lieutenant had doubled his coat under Obadiah's head and his face was pale as he looked up at Nathaniel. The latter saw in his eyes what his lips kept silent. The officer held something in his hand. It was the mysterious package which Captain Plum had taken his oath to deliver to the president of the United States.

"I don't dare move until the surgeon comes," said the lieutenant. "He wants to speak to you. I believe, if he has anything to say you had better hear it now."

His last words were in a whisper so low that Nathaniel scarcely heard them. As the lieutenant rose to his feet, he whispered again.

"He is dying!"

Obadiah's eyes opened as Nathaniel knelt beside him and from between his thin lips there came faintly the old, gurgling chuckle.

"Nat!" he breathed. His thin hand sought his companion's and clung to it tightly. "We have won. The vengeance of God — has come!"

In these last moments all madness had left the eyes of Obadiah Price.

"I want to tell you —" he whispered, and Nathaniel bent low. "I have given him the package. It is evidence I have gathered — all these years — to destroy the Mormon kingdom."

He tried to turn his head.

" Marion —" he whispered wistfully.

" She will come," said Nathaniel. " I will call her."

" No — not yet."

Obadiah's fingers tightened about Captain Plum's.

" I want to tell — you."

For a few moments he seemed struggling to command all his strength.

" A good many years ago," he said, as if speaking to himself, " I loved a girl — like Marion, and she loved me — as Marion loves you. Her people were Mormons, and they went to Kirtland — and I followed them. We planned to escape and go east, for my Jean was good and beautiful, and hated the Mormons as I hated them. But they caught us and — thought — they — killed —"

The old man's lips twitched and a convulsive shudder shook his body.

" When everything came back to me I was older — much older," he went on. " My hair

was white. I was like an old man. My people
had found me and they told me that I had been
mad for three years, Nat — mad — mad —
mad! and that a great surgeon had operated on
my head, where they struck me — and brought
me back to reason. Nat — Nat —" He
strained to raise himself, gasping excitedly.
" God, I was like you then, Nat! I went back
to fight for my Jean. She was gone. Nobody
knew me, for I was an old man. I hunted from
settlement to settlement. In my madness I became a Morman, for vengeance — in hope of
finding her. I was rich, and I became powerful.
I was made an elder because of my gold. Then
I found —"

A moan trembled on the old man's lips.

"— they had forced her to marry —·the son
of a Mormon —"

He stopped, and for a moment his eyes seemed
filling with the glazed shadows of death. He
roused himself almost fiercely.

" But he loved my Jean, Nat — he loved her

as I loved her — and he was a good man!" he whispered shrilly. "Quick — quick — I must tell you — they had tried to escape from Missouri and the Danites killed him,— and Joseph Smith wanted Jean and at the last moment she killed herself to save her honor — as — Marion — was going — to — do, and she left two children —"

He coughed and blood flecked his lips.

"She left — Marion and Neil!"

He sank back, ashen white and still, and with a cry Nathaniel turned to the lieutenant. The officer ran forward with a flask in his hand.

"Give him this!"

The touch of liquor to Obadiah's lips revived him. He whispered weakly.

"The children, Nat — I tried to find them — and years after — I did — in Nauvoo. The man and woman who had killed the father in their own house had taken them and were raising them as their own. I went mad! Vengeance — vengeance — I lived for it, year after year. I

316

wanted the children — but if I took them all would be lost. I followed them, watched them, loved them — and they loved me. I would wait — wait — until my vengeance would fall like the hand of God, and then I would free them, and tell them how beautiful their mother was. When Joseph Smith was killed and the split came the old folks followed Strang — and I — I too —"

He rested a moment, breathing heavily.

" I brought my Jean with me and buried her up there on the hill — the middle grave, Nat, the middle grave — Marion's mother."

Nathaniel pressed the liquor to the old man's lips again.

" My vengeance was at hand — I was almost ready — when Strang learned a part of the secret," he continued with an effort. " He found the old people were murderers. When Marion would not become his wife he told her what they had done. He showed her the evidence! He threatened them with death unless Marion became his wife. His sheriffs watched them night and day. He named the hour of their doom — unless Marion yielded to him. And to save them, her supposed parents — to keep the terrible knowledge of their crime from Neil — Marion — was — going — to — sacrifice — herself — when —"

Again he stopped. His breath was coming more faintly.

" I understand," whispered Nathaniel. " I understand —"

Obadiah's dimming eyes gazed at him steadily.

" I thought my vengeance would come — in time — to save her, Nat. But — it failed. I knew of one other way and when all seemed lost — I took it. I killed the old people — the murderers of her father — of my Jean! I knew that would destroy Strang's power —"

In a sudden spasm of strength he lifted his head. His voice came in a hoarse, excited whisper.

" You won't tell Marion — you won't tell Marion that I killed them —"

" No — never."

Obadiah fell back with a relieved sigh. After a moment he added.

" In a chest in the cabin there is a letter for Marion. It tells her about her mother — and the gold there — is for her — and Neil —"

His eyes closed. A shudder passed through his form.

" Marion —" he breathed. " Marion ! "

Nathaniel rose to his feet and ran to the cabin door.

" Marion ! " he called.

Blinding tears shut out the vision of the girl from his eyes. He pointed, looking from her, and she, knowing what he meant, sped past him to the old councilor.

In the great low room in which Obadiah Price had spent so many years planning his vengeance Captain Plum waited.

After a time, the girl came back.

There was great pain in her voice as she stretched out her arms to him blindly, sobbing his name.

" Gone — gone — they're all gone now — but Neil ! "

Nathaniel held out his arms.

" Only Neil,"— he cried, " only Neil — Marion —? "

" And you — you — you —"

Her arms were around his neck, he held her throbbing against his breast.

" And you —"

She raised her face, glorious in its love.

" If you want me — still."

And he whispered:

" For ever and for ever ! "

THE END